CROWN OF MIST AND HEAT

COURT OF BLOOD AND BINDING BOOK 2

MAGGIE ALABASTER

1

KHALA

"I'm listening."

Hours had passed since I said those words to Cavan, High Lord of the Summer Court. I still didn't have any answers. Ryze and Wornar had stepped through the portal and away. Ryze eased it closed behind him after giving me a long, worried glance.

All I could do was look back and nod. I'd be all right. I made my choice. I'd stay and hear Cavan out.

Cavan, expression smug as hells, had Dalyth hustle me off to living quarters in another part of the palace.

To my credit, I managed not to kill her on the way. The temptation was incredible after she wiped Zared's memory of the last couple of weeks and sent him back to Ebonfalls thinking I was living my best life in another temple somewhere.

Picturing the look on his face when Diana touched

him, the way she shoved him through the portal, was like a knife in my heart.

At the same time, in the back of my mind, was the niggling understanding it was the right thing to do. Zared would be better off without me. Without remembering I wasn't human anymore.

I hated that Dalyth did the one thing I was too much of a coward to do. Send him home. That knowledge was a twist of the knife. A searing pain I'd live with for the rest of my days. That same voice in the back of my mind suggested the person I should hate should be me, not the older Fae woman. I'd consider my subconscious' advice later.

"Your sisters will be along soon. They'll give you all the answers you need. Don't wander off." Dalyth gave me a smile like I was a child who might sneak into the kitchen and steal a cake before she left me in a wide, glass-ceilinged atrium.

The tiled floor was a pale stone I'd never seen before. Flecks of gold glittered in the sunlight that filtered through intricate lattice inset into the ceiling. The effect was that of a sparkling beach. Without the soothing lap of waves against the shore.

A variety of plants grew in pots that lined the walls: tall trees heavy with fruit, small plants dotted with dozens of flowers. Somehow they managed not to compete with each other for attention. Whoever chose their placement had a good eye. The result could have been a cluttered mess. Instead, it was a soothing garden in the top of a palace in a city. An oasis.

Low benches in stone darker than the floor, formed a ring around a circular reflecting pool placed in the centre of the atrium. Bright yellow fish darted across the water before they disappeared under lily pads covered with more flowers.

In spite of the sun coming in through both the ceiling and a picture window that overlooked the city and the harbour beyond, the atrium was comfortably cool

I could easily picture myself spending hours sitting on the benches reading a book or watching the fish. The space was serene. A moment of calm in a furious whirlwind.

That calm ended when the door opened and two women walked inside. They saw me standing beside the reflecting pool.

"Fuck," the taller one said.

She had Fae features now, like I did, but there was no mistaking the dark blonde hair and dark blue eyes.

Of course Hycanthe was one of the transformed omegas. Of *course* she fucking was.

The other was her dark-haired friend, Jezalyn.

"Khala." Jezalyn stepped toward me and took my

hands. Her dark brown eyes took in the sight of me. "I had no idea."

"None of us did," Hycanthe said sourly. She gave me an accusing look. "Unless you did and didn't tell anyone." Her eyes were narrowed slits, gaze angry and unwelcoming.

I couldn't stop myself from bristling. I understood she was looking for someone to blame, but this was as fucked up to me as it was to her.

I managed to keep my tone civil when I responded. "I'm as surprised as you are. Where's Tyla?" I already knew the answer, but I had to ask anyway. Five former Silent Maidens were sent to Havenmoor. The three of us standing in the atrium were the rest of a cohort of eight.

"They sent her back to Fraxius," Jezalyn confirmed. "She's human."

"Yes, she gets to go on with her life," Hycanthe said bitterly. "While we're stuck here, trying to make sense of it all."

"Dalyth said you'd have answers." I gently removed my hands from Jezalyn's and lowered myself down to one of the benches. The stone was cold under my ass.

Jezalyn sat beside me. "All we've been told is that the Summer Court sent out Fae alphas to Ebonfalls over twenty years ago to try to make more like us."

So this was going on longer than Ryze suspected. And deliberately.

"Cavan said he knew who my real parents were." My mind hadn't stopped racing since. Speculation, which ultimately led me nowhere. For all I knew, I should be calling him Daddy.

"They kept records," Jezalyn said. "They've been keeping track of us. That was how they knew to take us into the temple in the first place. Chances are, the name of your mother and whoever fathered you are in there."

I'd already come to terms that the man I thought of as my father probably wasn't. This might be as close to a confirmation as I might ever get.

"We might be actual sisters then," I said, half-joking. This whole situation was twisted as hells. Sometimes dark humour was the only way through.

Hycanthe gave me a look like she hoped not. The feeling was mutual.

"You can ask to see if you want to," Hycanthe said. "I didn't bother. It's just a name. It's meaningless."

"It was consensual," Jezalyn said to her.

"So they claim." Hycanthe wasn't appeased at all.

"You both went through heat?" I asked.

They glanced at each other.

Jezalyn's cheeks turned pink. "We did," she said carefully.

I looked from one to the other.

"Oh."

I smelled the different scents the moment they walked into the atrium, but I didn't realise the cause and significance until now.

"One of you is an alpha and the other is an omega." That would explain the sudden unease, and the way Jezalyn put herself between me and Hycanthe.

"I'm an alpha," Jezalyn said. "But I am a woman." Her chocolate brown eyes pleaded with me to understand, to not be judgemental.

"Of course you are," I said, light but firm. "You're my sister. Both of you." Even if Hycanthe hated my guts.

"We're a pack," Hycanthe growled. "Jezalyn and me."

I looked up at her evenly. "I have no intention of getting in the way of that. I have my own pack."

The mating bond I shared with them told me three were still in the city, but not nearby. The bond with Zared was stretched so thin, I was surprised it hadn't snapped. He was alive, but that was all I knew. Either he was too far away for me to sense what he was feeling, or he was still out cold from Dalyth tampering with his memories.

"What are you doing here, then?" Jezalyn asked pointedly.

I glanced towards the door. Fae hearing being what

it was, the guards outside might be listening to everything we said. Instead of speaking out loud, I used the Silent Maiden's hand language. One we were all too familiar with.

I briefly told them about Ryze's suspicion that Cavan was trying to mess with the weather, leaving Jorius in permanent summer. And then about his aspirations to take all of Jorius from the other three Fae courts.

"I came in here to look for you and try to get you out," I signed finally. "So he can't use you for whatever magic you have. You and any other former Silent Maidens who might be here. It's not just you two, is it?" From what Ryse believed, there had to be more than the three of us.

"There are six more," Jezalyn said. "Three from the year before us and three from the year before that. It seems to be a magic number." She didn't seem convinced it was anything more than coincidence.

I frowned, but couldn't see any particular significance either. It may be nothing more magical than luck. Or the gods' sense of humour. They seemed to like fucking with Fae and humans alike.

Hycanthe frowned. "You came here to get us out? Why?"

"Like I said, I don't want Cavan to use you for your magic. Do you have any?"

Whatever I pictured coming here, this wasn't it. At the least, I'd expected to find Tyla here. We'd hug each other, then find a way to get out of the city. I hadn't let myself think beyond that moment. I hadn't, I admitted, thought about what might have happened to Zared.

The plan, which he strenuously objected to, was for him to stay with the other men and for me to come here alone. We'd misjudged how long it would take Cavan's people to find us. It was a small mercy they hadn't killed him on sight. Or when we arrived here, at the palace. Sending him home was unexpected and unwelcome at the time. In retrospect, it was the least of several evils they could have inflicted on him.

Still, the blank expression on his face was seared into my soul forever.

I forced the thought aside for now. If I let it linger in my mind too much, I was going to cry. The time for that would come later.

Hycanthe ignored the question. "You came here because you didn't know it was us. You thought Tyla was here, or you wouldn't have come. Would you?"

The glance Jezalyn gave her omega was the most alpha-like expression I'd ever seen on her face. It reminded me so much of Ryze, my heart twinged.

I hadn't entirely forgiven him for lying to me, for not telling me I may transform into Fae, but he was still my alpha, a part of my pack. He'd agreed to let me come, orchestrating the situation to look like Cavan took me against my will.

"You and I haven't always gotten along," I signed. "But Ryze is convinced Cavan is planning something that will end up in an all-out war. I came here because I care about my sisters and because I don't want hundreds, thousands of people to die."

"Sounds like a no to me," Hycanthe muttered out loud.

"Hycanthe has magic," Jezalyn signed. "I don't. All the omegas here do. To varying degrees of skill."

Hycanthe huffed.

"I'm still learning to use mine too." There was no shame in my admission that I needed the practice.

"I almost set one of the guards on fire," Hycanthe said, as though throwing down a challenge.

"I almost drowned one of my lovers because I couldn't make an ice bridge properly," I said.

She pursed her lips and sighed.

I think I won that round.

I cocked my head at Hycanthe. "You have Summer Court magic. Have you tried to open a portal?"

"Yes." She shrugged. "They made Jezalyn order me not to make one without Cavan's permission."

"It stayed open?" I asked. "You could walk through it?"

Hycanthe looked confused. "Yes. Isn't that the point?"

"Supposedly." I briefly explained that mine snapped shut before I could step through, and the sensation that something was missing with my magic.

"Maybe you should stay here," Hycanthe said. "That High Lord of yours doesn't seem like a good teacher to me."

I shifted uncomfortably at her criticism of Ryze. "It's not that. I just...need to work on it. That's all."

Hycanthe smirked.

"Do you have any idea what Cavan is up to?" I signed.

Jezalyn shook her head. "We haven't seen much of him since we arrived. Mostly, we see Dalyth. She's the one who teaches the omegas how to use their magic."

"Has she taught you how to change people's memories?" I asked Hycanthe.

"No. Not beyond watching her do it to Tyla and the other sisters." Hycanthe flopped down onto the bench on the other side of Jezalyn. "Mostly I spend my time lighting candles." She curled her lip.

"Lighting candles is a useful skill," Jezalyn told her. "I can't do it." She shot her omega an affectionate look.

"You two transitioned at the same time," I realised. "That must have been horrible." Mine was bad enough and I had Zared and Tavian to cool me down, and Ryze and Vayne to watch over me. All they had was each other.

Jezalyn laced her fingers in Hycanthe's. "It wasn't easy. I kept telling the staff to look after her, but she wouldn't let any of them touch her."

"I wanted them to look after you too," Hycanthe argued. "They *were* the strangers who kidnapped us from the caravan."

After a moment, and while she was looking at Jezalyn like she was the only other person in the world, Hycanthe added, "And because they weren't you."

I glanced away, uncomfortable at witnessing a tender moment between them. I felt as though I was intruding.

"But we got through." Jezalyn looked back at me. "You really think we'll be safer in the Winter Court? They haven't mistreated us here. Although, we're not allowed to leave."

"We've gone from one gilded cage to another," Hycanthe said bitterly. "But I need to learn to use my magic. If I did anything to hurt Jezalyn—"

"You wouldn't," Jezalyn assured her. "I wouldn't let you." She sighed softly. "We'll have to think about it. For all we know, your information might be wrong, and if it's not, we might be able to do something from here. There's a lot to consider."

"Consider quickly," I signed. "We won't have long."

In case Hycanthe decided to be difficult, I added, "I will go into heat again at some point. It would be better for everyone if that didn't happen here."

It certainly wasn't going to happen with Jezalyn. I was quite sure Cavan had alphas at his disposal and mine, but it wouldn't hurt to push the other omega a little.

"Don't make me set you on fire," Hycanthe growled.

"Don't make me freeze your brain," I retorted. I hadn't tried doing that to anyone yet, but it was better if she didn't tempt me. Just in case.

Not to mention the fact she wasn't my enemy. The sooner she realised it, the better.

2

───────────

KHALA

he atrium door swung open on silent hinges. Dalyth strode inside like she was High Lady of the Summer Court.

"I see you've found each other," she said smoothly.

Her citrus and honey scent tickled my nostrils uncomfortably. If I was going to freeze anyone's brain, it would be hers. She gave me the creeps. What she did to Zared, clearly gave her pleasure. Fucking with humans as though somehow they were lesser than Fae, was ugly. And misinformed.

"I don't think we so much as found each other as were directed here." I rose and looked at her steadily. I had a ton of questions I wanted to ask, but I doubted she'd be forthcoming.

"I'm sure you're wondering why." She walked over to a tree full of apricots and pulled off one of the fruit.

She was an omega too. I smelled it on her. I hadn't realised the scent was so distinct until now. It was like a cake baking in the oven, and soft lavender. Smells which should be warm, sweet and comforting. On her, they competed with her natural scent.

Judging by the way Jezalyn raised her nose and inhaled, it was a pleasing scent to an alpha.

What would a beta make of it?

"The thought crossed my mind." I stood my ground, even when she looked at me like she could see through me. Her eyes seemed to bore into my soul.

"You would know by now the Summer Court has been working for some time to make people like us," she said smoothly. She bit into the apricot and chewed.

Us? She was a transformed omega too?

"I see I took you by surprise," she said after she swallowed. "You didn't realise I know exactly what you went through. I absolutely do. The pain of the change. Feeling like your whole body is being ripped apart. Torn to shreds before being put back together."

She took another fierce bite, shredding the fruit in the same way she was shredded.

"What difference does it make?" I asked. "You still took my sisters from the caravan and brought them here. You changed Zared's memories. Sent him to a place he didn't want to be." A place that was best for him, but that he didn't want. He made it more than clear that, wherever I was, he belonged there too. She'd taken that choice from him. From us. Stripped it away like it was nothing.

"You truly think he'd want to be here?" She swept her hand around the atrium. "Amongst Fae. Amongst alphas and omegas. Knowing he would never be any of those things. You claim to care about him. If you do, then you will realise I did him a favour. The same way I did your sisters a favour. Her heat—" she nodded toward Hycanthe "—was as inevitable as yours. As inevitable as mine. If she'd undergone that in Havenmoor, if you had, what do you think would have happened? With no alpha for you, you wouldn't have survived. If by some miracle you had, do you think the humans there would have let any of you live?"

"You don't know that there are no alphas there," I stated.

"Don't I?" She raised an eyebrow at me. She finished her apricot and tossed the stone into the base of a pot.

"Do you think that isn't something I'd look into? That Cavan wouldn't have looked into? Ryze too. I promise you, there were no alphas there apart from Jezalyn. My spies in the Winter Court say you went into heat shortly after Hycanthe. You would have gone through yours while she and Jezalyn transitioned. In the event everyone was in agreement, Jezalyn would have been unable to help you. Hycanthe's heat triggered her transition as well as her own. Jezalyn might have *tried* to help you, instinctively, but that would have killed her. Mid-transition is the most dangerous time."

Dalyth took a couple of steps towards me. "So, you see, you couldn't have stayed with the caravan or the Temple. Until we knew exactly who was an omega, or an alpha, we had to bring you to a safe place. Safe for everyone."

"Great." I raised my hands and dropped them to my sides. "We're safe. You won't mind if we leave now."

"I do mind," she said. "Hycanthe has yet to learn how to use her magic properly. I'd bet you haven't either."

I didn't have to answer, the twitch of my mouth told her everything she needed to know.

"I thought so. I can teach you how to use it."

"Why would you do that?" I asked. What the hells was in it for her?

"Like I said, I know exactly what you went through." Her voice was low now, soothing. Like an omega who wanted her alpha to buy her expensive jewelry. Like she was trying to convince me she was my friend.

"We have something else in common. A combination of hot and cold. My father was a Fae from the

Summer Court. I spent my transition heat with an alpha from the Winter Court."

She looked sly, clearly trying to convince me she spent her first heat with Ryze. He'd mentioned knowing her, but never said how. Had they really—

That was a mental image I did *not* want in my brain. If anything, it made me want to freeze hers even more. I was pissed off with him, but he was still mine.

I pushed away my annoyance and shrugged. "So what?"

"So, when you try to use magic, you feel like something is missing, don't you? The power is there, but there's some key element that isn't in place. Another reason you should have been here for your heat. It's much easier to manage one type of magic than trying to combine two. If you'd had your transition heat with Cavan instead, your magic would be perfectly aligned."

"What is Hycanthe's?" I asked. Her heat took place here, but with two part Fae-part humans taking part, things might be different again.

"We're not sure," Dalyth admitted. "We only know of one other transitioned alpha. It's definitely had an impact on her magic." She shot both women a quick glance, accusing or frustrated. Either way, it didn't seem like it fit into Cavan's plans.

Excuse me if I didn't feel bad about that.

"It seems to me like you're messing with something

you shouldn't be messing with," I said. "Why start all of this in the first place?"

Her expression shut down immediately. "All you need to know is I'll train you to use your magic. You'll stay here with the other omegas. And before you think it, the atrium is warded against anyone making a portal in or out. There are guards on the door all the time. For your safety, of course."

I snorted. "Of course." Hycanthe was right. From one gilded cage to another. Only this cage, I had no intention of staying in. Not a moment longer than I had to.

She smiled as though there was no hint of sarcasm in my tone. I doubted she missed it. She was too astute for that. She was the kind of woman who didn't miss much.

"Good, I'll be back first thing in the morning to start your lessons. You'll find a spare nest in the room at the end. Make yourself comfortable. You're a member of the Summer Court now. Don't worry, we'll ensure a suitable alpha is ready for your next heat. Cavan himself, if you're lucky."

Lucky wasn't the word I was thinking of. Like Ryze, Cavan had Fae arrogance to spare. He was fully aware of his power. That made him both compelling and extremely dangerous.

"Wonderful." There was more of my sarcasm. "I can't wait."

"Of course you can't," she said, all honey and light. "It's an honour to be chosen by a High Lord." She seemed to believe every word she was saying. Maybe she did. She was welcome to all of them except Ryze. Especially Harel. The High Lord of Autumn gave me the creeps even more than she did.

She swept out of the room without another word, closing the door firmly behind her.

Hycanthe made a rude sound under her breath. "I can't stand that woman. If she got the chance, she'd separate Jezalyn and me and throw me at whatever alpha she thinks I should fuck."

"I won't let her separate us," Jezalyn said, curling her fingers around Hycanthe's. "You're mine and I'm yours, and that's that."

"We should get out of here before she tries," I said. "Neither of us like the idea of being offered up to some strange alpha. Whatever it is they want with us and our magic, that's bad enough. What if they decide to go further? I don't think either of us wants to be bred to make some super-powerful Fae or whatever shit they might think."

My stomach turned at the thought.

"I'd sooner throw myself out the window," Hycanthe declared. "Or set myself on fire. Or let Khala freeze my brain." She could have gone on for hours, but we understood.

None of us wanted to be bred against our will. I hoped my mother felt something for the Fae man who impregnated her. That was something I wouldn't dwell on too much, because that was a question I may never get the answer to.

What I remembered of the people who raised me, they were warm towards each other, loving. However I came about, they had that. Did they still have it? I hoped they did. In spite of offering me up to the Temple, I wanted them to be happy. They were my parents, as far as I was concerned.

"Dalyth is right about one thing," Jezalyn said slowly. "You both should learn how to use your magic properly. For your safety, for everyone else's safety, and because we might need it if we have to run from here."

I hated to admit it, but she was right. If I had a combination of magic the way Dalyth said, the way Wornar and Ryze surmised, then I needed someone from the Summer Court to teach me. I'd have to let Dalyth do that. For a little while anyway.

I nodded. "All right, we'll stay for a while. Until we get a handle on everything. Then we make our plans. We get out of here, together."

I looked from one of my sisters to the other. Of all the Silent Maidens my age, these were the two I knew the least. By the time this was over, that will have changed. Not to mention the fact we all now had a few hundred years together.

In the back of my mind was a kernel of disappointment that I wouldn't share that with Tyla. She and I would have been laughing about all of this by now.

If we both agreed to stay for a little while longer, we would have made the most of it.

Instead, she was getting on with her human life like Zared was. Becoming a priestess and assuming I was living in some other temple, happy, and also human.

Would she write me letters and send them? She might. When she didn't get a reply, she'd eventually stop. She might assume I didn't want to be her friend anymore. Or that I met an attractive priest that consumed all my time outside of work.

She'd never know what really happened to me. That reality settled heavily on my heart. Her life would pass in the blink of my eye, then she'd be gone forever.

I wiped a tear off my cheek before the other women noticed. Not before sending sadness down the bond, apparently. I got a surge of reassurance back from Ryze and Tavian. And something from Vayne that felt like the emotional equivalent of a grunt. That was about all I could expect from the grumpy Fae commander. He wasn't chatty, but he got his point across.

I sent thanks back and assurances that I was all right. I wished I could send words and receive them. I would have liked to hear their voices right now. To explain the conversation I had with Hycanthe and Jezalyn. I'd even be happy to hear Vayne grumbling about whatever he was grumbling about in the moment.

Right now, I'd give just about anything to be curled up in my nest with them.

3

KHALA

Hycanthe slumped on the bench beside Jezalyn while Dalyth talked me through everything she probably learned weeks ago.

The other omegas had shared a quick breakfast with us before being hustled away somewhere else. No one explained where and I didn't bother to ask. They wouldn't have told me anyway.

I recognised a couple of them from the Temple in Fraxius. I'd take them with me when I left, if I could. I didn't think for a minute any of them were here of their own free will. Truthfully, the temptation to leave immediately was great, but the need to learn how to use my magic was greater.

"Now, focus on the water and the fire," Dalyth instructed. "Think of them like two threads coming together to form a blanket. Weave them together."

I saw how to draw the magic out of the water. I could have frozen the whole reflecting pool, or formed it into tiny drops of ice. From the fire, however, all I felt was warmth with a trace of magic. Nothing more. Nothing that wanted to work for me or with me.

I placed a hand over both and tried again. A fountain of water rose up from the pool, only to splash back down.

"Try again," Dalyth ordered. She was clearly getting frustrated.

So was I.

"Maybe I'm not what you think I am," I told her. "I might only have an affinity with winter."

"Maybe you just need some help," Dalyth said stubbornly.

She waved Jezalyn over. "Order her to channel both kinds of magic." She looked pissed at having to ask an alpha for help. Maybe she wished she was one.

Jezalyn gave me an apologetic look, then cleared her throat. "Channel both kinds of magic," she told me in a very alpha tone she clearly wasn't used to using. Under other circumstances, we might have giggled about it.

Today, I felt the weight of her command, and Hycanthe's glare. The omega in me was eager to obey. Not as eager as it was to obey Ryze, but eager enough. Like a puppy happy to wag her tail and sit for a treat.

I stretched my hands out and half closed my eyes.

The water rose out of the pool and danced under my fingertips. Smoke rose from the fire and became thicker.

"Combine them," Dalyth urged. "Make the magic do what you want it to do."

Considering I wanted to incinerate her, I thought I should probably ignore that advice.

I focused instead on a small plant at the edge of the garden. Carefully, carefully I nudged it with warmth and moisture. After a moment, it started to grow. Tendrils curled out from the sides and grew buds. The buds burst open, becoming vibrantly coloured flowers. The plant grew a metre, two metres.

In a blink, the whole plant wilted and slumped into a pile of wet, brown stalks and petals.

"You need to learn some restraint," Dalyth scolded. "However, we now know you have some ability, in spite of yourself. Try again."

I did, but all I managed to do was to make the reflecting pool bubble and steam. When I cooled it, it turned to slush. I thawed that quickly, but not quickly enough for the fish, whose tiny, dead, yellow bodies floated to the surface.

Dalyth sighed. "Take a break. Hycanthe, it's your turn."

I flopped down beside Jezalyn on the bench and watched Hycanthe try to light a candle in front of her.

"It's not your fault," Jezalyn said softly. When I glanced at her she added, "The fish. Or the plant. You tried. You just need to tie the tendrils of magic together more closely. You have them too loose, like a stitch that needs to be pulled firmer."

I stared at her, but forced my eyes away before Dalyth noticed.

"You can see magic?"

"I think I might be the only one who can," she whispered. "No one else has ever said anything about it."

I glanced over to Hycanthe, but I saw absolutely nothing.

"You can see hers?"

Jezalyn gave a tiny nod. "Hers isn't as strong as yours. She has the control, but she needs to work harder to do smaller things. She gets stronger every time she tries. I think that scares her. If it keeps getting stronger, how strong might it get?"

"Strong enough that she might accidentally hurt you someday?" I suggested. "But she might need to be strong to protect you."

"I think she's worried she won't be strong enough," Jezalyn whispered. "She's tough on the outside. On the inside, she's terrified."

"I know how she feels," I said. I didn't want to hurt anyone unnecessarily either.

I also wasn't convinced I could combine the two magics successfully. They felt too opposite, like night and day. They wanted to work against each other, not in unity.

I wished I'd taken the time to ask Wornar about his. Both the Spring and Autumn Courts used a combination of both magics. Only Summer and Winter used one or the other. Maybe that was the problem. In order to use both, I had to have Spring or Autumn Court blood, or to have had my first heat in one of them.

Instead, I stood on the bridge between two opposing courts. A bridge either made out of ice or fire. Since I couldn't successfully make a bridge of ice and didn't like the idea of trying to walk on one made of fire, I was stuck in the middle.

Hycanthe tentatively lit the candle over and over. Every time she succeeded, Dalyth put it out with a flick of her finger.

"Is she using magic for that?" I asked.

"Yes," Jezalyn replied. "A tiny string of heat and cold. It looks like a whisper of wind."

Her words echoed in my mind for a moment, going around and around. Something clicked into place that hadn't before. An understanding. I could actually see what I needed to do.

I half closed my eyes and drew heat from the fire to warm the ground in front of me. At the same time, I used water to cool the air. As the warm air rose, the cool air rushed in underneath it, creating an eddy of wind. It swirled around, making the leaves on the plants quiver and rustle.

It grew. The wind whistled, then howled. The flame on the candle flickered and danced. Smaller plants and branches whipped this way and that.

I barely managed to tug the wind back before it tore them out by their roots. I snuck in a bit more warmth, drops at a time, until a gentle, cool breeze blew through the atrium, soft like spring.

Only when I let the breeze drop, did I realise all three women were staring at me. Jezalyn with awe. Hycanthe with annoyance.

Dalyth looked impressed. "We may have something to work with after all. You even showed restraint."

"I saw what to do and I did it," I said, trying to sound indifferent. I didn't want her praise. Didn't want to feel good about pleasing her.

"That was incredible," Jezalyn said. "Just what this place needs, a nice breeze."

Her praise, on the other hand, warmed my omega heart.

The expression on Hycanthe's face was a bucket of ice, bringing me back down to earth.

"Thanks," I muttered. Even as I was enjoying her praise, I wanted to hear those words from Ryze. I wanted to see his usual smug amusement turn to admiration and pride. I needed him to tell me how amazing I was until all I could do was purr in response.

"Wind isn't very useful, is it, though?" Hycanthe said.

It would be if I wanted to knock her on her ass, but I just clasped my hands in my lap. "I guess not."

"Let's see if you can make something grow," Dalyth said to Hycanthe. They moved away to the edge of the atrium, to a pot in the corner.

"If she didn't hate my guts before, she does now," I said softly. I wasn't sure why it mattered. Hycanthe and I survived ten years of not getting along with each other. We could survive a lifetime.

"That's her insecurity talking," Jezalyn whispered. "I'd bet anything she wished she could do that too."

"She can do that better than I can." I nodded over to where Hycanthe was making a tomato plant grow from almost nothing, into a vine.

I stared.

In the back of my mind, a memory awakened. Slowly at first, then in a rush, like the river after the ice wall collapsed.

Not a tomato plant, but corn. My mother had nurtured seedlings in the potting shed. Dozens of them. She and my father had carried them out of the shed and planted them in neat rows in the dirt. I'd helped them, for hours, getting dirtier and dirtier, but loving every moment. After all the seedlings were safely planted in the ground, they told me to go and play.

I'd run off, but rather than playing like they said, something made me stop and hide behind the wagon. I crouched down and peered between the wheels. Watched as my mother knelt in the dirt beside the seedlings.

One by one, she made them grow. In a minute or two, several were a couple of metres tall. Cobs already grew off them, encased in their green sheath.

This was like something out of the stories my grandmother told me while I was sitting on her lap. Tales of magic and Fae. That was all I thought they were. Until that moment.

Then, I couldn't comprehend what I saw.

I snuck out from behind the wagon to get a closer look.

She must have seen my movement, because she turned to me.

I couldn't remember her face, not clearly, but I remembered the way her hair always hung over her ears. I remembered how her face paled. Turned angry.

"Khala, go inside," she snarled.

I'd never seen her so furious. She raised a hand as though she was going to hit me. I let out a squeak, and turned and ran. I scurried into our house and hid under the table.

I stayed there until it was almost dark and my mother came in to start preparing the evening meal. Neither of us ever said a word about what I saw.

I must have pushed it out of my mind until now. What did it mean? My mother was Fae? Was the man I thought of as my father, my father after all?

She used to say her ears were scarred, from an accident, that was why she covered them with her hair. She refused to elaborate. Had I ever seen them? I didn't think so. If I had, I would have remembered seeing them end in a point. I was certain now that they would.

If they didn't, then she or someone else had done something to them. Rounded the tips so she could pass as human, perhaps. Gods, how had I forgotten all of this? What did it mean that I was remembering it now?

"Khala? Are you all right?" Jezalyn asked. "You're white as snow."

I blinked a couple of times, reorienting myself. I was in the atrium, in Garial, in the Summer Court.

"I'm fine," I said quickly. "Too much Winter Court magic maybe." I gave a short, humourless laugh.

She looked at me like she didn't believe me, but

wouldn't press the issue. Not in front of Dalyth. Maybe not in front of Hycanthe either.

I appreciated that. I needed time to think. My mother must have been an omega, if she had magic. If she could make corn grow like that, then chances were she wasn't from the Winter Court. Summer Court would be my guess. Dalyth had the combination right, but not the order. I didn't have a Fae father.

If I did, I'd look Fae from birth. At least, that was my understanding. The man I thought of as my father was actually my father. My mother must have given up her life in Jorius to be with him. She must have truly loved him. If anything was going to warm my omega heart, it was that.

"Where are those records of who we are?" I asked.

"There's a library across the corridor from the atrium," Jezalyn said.

"Yes there is," Dalyth said. She must have finished her lesson with Hycanthe and approached when I was lost in my memory. She was standing only a couple of metres away now. "You may use it with permission from Cavan or myself, but I don't have time right now. I have other duties to attend to. As does he," she added as though one of us was about to suggest the High Lord would bother to take the time to show us around the library.

"I'm sure you must be busy," I said. Probably doing

something like sucking Cavan's cock. I kept that thought to myself. The visual image was bad enough.

"Very," she agreed. She gave us all a nod and swept out of the room with that High Lady of the Summer Court air of hers.

I suspected she wished that was exactly what she was.

4

KHALA

The door clicked shut behind Dalyth, leaving the three of us alone. Jezalyn turned to me, a stern expression on her face.

"All right, what was going on with you? People don't usually go white when they watch plants grow."

"Plants don't usually grow that quickly," I pointed out. "I was overwhelmed."

She gave me a look of flat disbelief. "Bullshit. Don't make me order you to tell me."

"She's not your omega," Hycanthe said darkly, her ire clearly aimed at me. "She's not part of our pack."

"No, I'm not." I stood and moved away from them both, then turned and briefly told them about my memory.

"That's all. To the surprise of no one, I'm part Fae."

"How did you remember what happened before

you went to the temple?" Jezalyn asked. "I don't remember anything."

"Neither do I." A frown was etched on Hycanthe's brow. "I figured it was just me until they changed the memories of our other sisters."

Jezalyn nodded at her. "Right. We figured they must have changed ours before we went to the temple, so we couldn't remember our lives before."

I gaped. That made way more sense than it probably should. "I don't know. Maybe they left gaps. Or they changed the bits after this memory." I had no idea how old I was when I saw my mother make the corn grow, so it was possible.

"Neither of you remember anything before Ebonfalls?"

"Nothing," Jezalyn said. "Not one thing." She glanced down towards the floor uneasily.

I had a thought that made my blood run cold. "Do you think they do the same to our families? Make them forget us?" I'd waited all those years, hoping mine might drop in to visit, or send me a letter. Was the only reason they hadn't, because they didn't remember me at all?

Jezalyn's gaze shot back up. She exchanged furious glances with her omega. Neither dismissed the suggestion. I wasn't expecting them to.

"Jezalyn, did you see what Dalyth did to change

their memories?" I asked.

"I did, but it looked complicated," she said slowly. "Like several strands of magic were involved."

I'd have to try to figure out a way to have multiple strands going. It would be a lot easier if I could see what Jezalyn saw, but at least she could tell me if I was close. I doubted it was a skill Dalyth would teach me, or one Ryze *could* teach me.

No, I might have to figure this one out for myself.

"Ryze said some skills are advanced magic," I said slowly. " It seems like the more kinds of magic a Fae has access to, the more complicated it becomes."

"I wonder if any Fae is one quarter of each court," Hycanthe said. "According to Dalyth, Autumn and Spring are combined but opposite to each other. Autumn needs more cold than warmth, and Spring is the other way around. She said my magic is like spring, but I can't access the cold, so it comes off weaker."

"And Khala's is a solid combination of Summer and Winter," Jezalyn said. "Like Dalyth's."

I wrinkled my nose at the idea of having anything in common with that woman.

"I bet Dalyth is pissed you didn't have your first heat here," Hycanthe said to me. "She seems to have a lot more time for the omegas who are strong in Summer Court magic. It sounds like you'd be her new favourite." For some reason, she seemed to find that idea funny. Her eyes shone with humour.

"Lucky I didn't then," I said dryly. I stepped over to the reflecting pool and looked down at the poor, dead fish. They lay with their eyes open, probably staring accusingly at me.

"Don't feel too bad about them, they've only been there a few days," Hycanthe said. "I might have boiled the water and killed the last lot. I don't know why they bothered replacing them."

"To remind you to have some self-control," Jezalyn told her. "You didn't do it again, did you?"

"No, that was all me," I said, my eyes still on the pool. I crouched and reached out my finger to one of the fish.

Without thinking, I drew a little warmth from what was left of the fire and mixed it with a sliver of cold to make some air. I pushed a drop through the fish's gills. Just lightly, I touched the fish with my fingertips.

The moment my skin touched its scales, it flicked its tail and darted away under the lily pads.

"Holy shit," Hycanthe said. "You just—" She crouched beside me, eyes huge. "Can you teach me how to do that?"

I didn't have the heart to tell her she needed a touch of Winter Court magic. I glanced over my shoulder at Jezalyn, who nodded. It would be our secret.

"Just give the fish some warmth," I said. For once, I resisted the urge to dig or tease. This was a moment between sisters. The first step in building bridges between us.

As she reached out to do as I said, I slid in some cold. A moment later, the other fish darted away to join the first one.

"You think we can do that with people?" She looked awed.

"I have no idea," I admitted. "I'm not even sure how we did that to begin with." Like with the wind, I saw how to do it and did it. I didn't have a clue it would actually work.

Whoever heard of fish being brought back to life?

I rose and wiped my brow. "When did it get so hot in here?" The sun shone through the window when we started. It wasn't now and inside the atrium was hotter than before. Nearly uncomfortably so.

"That always happens," Jezalyn said. "The more anyone practices magic in here, the hotter it gets. It'll cool down soon."

"Or sooner," I said. This I could do. Just a little water, cooled down with ice, infused into the air, and the temperature dropped almost immediately.

"I wish I could do that," Hycanthe sighed. "Or better

yet, get out of here and go down to the ocean for a swim. Or sit on the waterfront and enjoy the sea air. I never thought I'd miss Ebonfalls, but I do. We had more freedom there."

"We couldn't talk to each other," Jezalyn said. "Not out loud, anyway."

"We got by." Hycanthe gave her a soft look. "There are worse things than not being able to use our voices. At least we could communicate with each other. Otherwise, I think we all would have gone completely crazy."

She was right there. When we'd arrived at the temple as eight-year-olds, trying to understand each other was hells until we learned how to speak with our hands. Now I thought about it, we learned pretty quickly, out of sheer necessity.

"Plus, it's useful when we don't want to be overheard," I signed.

"That too," Hycanthe signed back.

Since we were getting along for a moment, I ventured to ask, "Have you tried using cold magic?"

"Of course I have," she snapped. Apparently our moment of truce was over. "What do you think I've been doing all these weeks?"

"I have no fucking idea," I snapped back. "I don't think your magic is working the way it should. Either you haven't tried everything or you're not trying hard enough."

What was it about her that always made me have the need to bite back? I was never able to walk away from an argument with her, even when the last thing I wanted to do was argue. Some days it was all I could do to resist slapping her silly. Right now, that would get us absolutely nowhere. And Jezalyn would be stuck in the middle of it, which she didn't deserve. What she saw in Hycanthe, I had no idea. Love was blind, I supposed. It was yet another example of the gods' humour.

"Khala—" Jezalyn said in warning.

"No," I said back. "You said yourself she gets stronger every time she tries. She had no trouble getting the magic she needed a moment ago with that fish."

"You're one to talk," Hycanthe said. "You only seem able to do what you want to do when you feel like it. That's what you're saying about me, isn't it?"

I sucked in a breath. I supposed I was.

"If we're going to get out of here, we need to get a handle on this. Both of us. Jezalyn doesn't think your magic is weak, and neither do I. Maybe we both have a problem with authority figures, and being told what to do. We need to get past that and learn."

"I don't think so," Jezalyn said. "In fact, it might be best not to show Dalyth what you can do. I think both of you know that, but you haven't realised it. Neither of you trust her. I can't blame you for that. She killed a bunch of priests and kidnapped us. That's not something a trustworthy person does. I think both of you have a block where she's concerned. I think you should keep having it."

I chewed my lip for a moment. "You're right. I definitely don't want to do big things in front of her. That wind was probably a bad idea."

"It's a really good thing she didn't see those fish then," Hycanthe said.

I winced. "She can't see them alive." I didn't want to kill the poor things twice. That seemed so unfair. All they were doing was trying to live their best fishy lives. I mean, this was no river or lake, but it was pleasant enough.

"We don't have a choice," Jezalyn said. "We need to get rid of them, but we can put them in the toilet and hope they reach the ocean."

"They might stand a chance then." I never thought I'd be standing in the Summer Court having a conversation about putting fish down the toilet. Ryze would have found it hilarious. Tavian too. As for Zared, he would have shook his head, snatched the fish out of the water, and let them die in his hand. Whatever it took to keep us safe.

I stood back while both women grabbed bowls and started chasing the fish around the pool. Under any other circumstances, it would have been hilarious.

Right now, I had too many thoughts chasing themselves around my brain.

The memory of my mother. The fact I had memories at all. Most of all, the need to practice as much as I could away from Dalyth's gaze. The sooner I had a handle on things, the sooner we could get the fuck out of here.

I winced at the realisation I'd have to tell Tavian what Dalyth and Harel did to Zared. He was going to be as devastated as I was. If I didn't kill Dalyth, he probably would. I might let him do it.

The moment I thought about the Master of Assassins, I realised I felt him strongly through the bond. He was close. What the hells was he up to?

5

———————

KHALA

The nest dipped. Someone slid in beside me. A hand clamped down over my mouth, muffling my startled squeak.

"Shhh, it's me," Tavian whispered in my ear. He took his hand off my mouth.

"Fucking hells, you scared the crap out of me," I whispered. "How did you get in here?"

His teeth flashed white in the darkness. "Assassin training. No one saw me come in. If they did, they'd be dead right now. Ryze prefers I don't make a mess if I can help it. Sometimes I listen. Depends on my mood."

I noticed that about him. "Why are you here?" I asked.

He slid a hand down my cheek. "Why do you think? I was pissed Ryze let you come. Especially without telling Vayne and me. Vayne is pissed too."

"When is he not?" I asked.

Tavian chuckled. "Good point. But this time I thought he might punch Ryze in the face. He doesn't like people keeping secrets from him."

"I know the feeling," I said meaningfully.

He sighed, his breath brushing my cheek. "If I could have told you, I would have. I'll find a way to make it up to you." He sounded regretful but sincere. Clearly he was no happier with the situation than Vayne was. Than I was.

If he wanted to help, I could think of a couple of ways he could do that.

"You're good at sneaking," I said slowly. "Could you get into the library across the corridor? According to Hycanthe and Jezalyn, there are records there about us. The Silent Maidens-turned omega Fae."

"You want me to find the record on you?" he asked, like it was no big deal for him to do that. "Give me a few minutes. I'll be right back."

His teeth flashed again. The bed rose as he snuck away. It was no wonder he'd crept up on me while I was sleeping. I knew he was there, and I still couldn't hear him. All I made out was a low shadow slipping out the door.

I lay in the darkness and watched the twinkling stars out the window. The same stars that shone over

Ebonfalls. Was Zared looking at them too, or was he fast asleep? I couldn't feel anything down the bond apart from a faint presence. He was alive, that was all.

I missed him like an ache in my chest. As the saying went, you never know the blessings the gods give you until they take them away. I knew I cared about him, but I didn't know how deeply that ran until now. Until it was too late to tell him. If I had told him, he wouldn't remember the words anyway. I would have, though. That would have been something. Instead, all I had was regret. Regret I'd probably feel for a very, very long time.

"I'm sorry," I whispered into the darkness. The only answer was silence.

The bed dipped again a couple of minutes later. I barely managed to contain a startled gasp.

"I found it," Tavian whispered. "I didn't read it. I thought you'd want to." He pressed what felt like a few sheets of paper into my hand.

"People will notice if I turn on a light, so I'll need a candle," I said. I made no move to get up and get one. Not yet. Something else was more pressing than that.

Fuck, the words were difficult.

"What is it?" he whispered. "You don't want to know what those say?"

"I do," I said quickly. "That's not it. It's about Zared."

Gods, I didn't know if I could do this. I had to. I swallowed down my emotions and tried to order my thoughts.

"I know what they did," Tavian said softly. "You told me through the bond. Not the specific details, but enough. They returned him to Fraxius."

I sniffed back tears. "They took his memories, then they sent him back. They said it was best for him if he didn't remember ever being in Jorius. He won't remember you. Ryze, or Vayne. Or that I changed to a Fae. Or that he and I ever..."

Tavian drew me into his arms and rubbed my back, letting me cry silently.

While I wept, he said soothing things in my ear, like, "They're assholes. We'll deal with them." And, "I'll sneak in and assassinate Cavan right now if you want? We probably won't get out of here alive, but I'll do it for you."

By the time my tears ran dry, I was almost able to smile. Only he could cheer me with suggestions of cold-blooded murder.

"As tempting as that is, I don't want both of us to get killed." I went to wipe away my tears, but the moment my warm skin got to within a centimetre of my face, they dried. I was barely aware of doing it.

"We'll figure something out," he said. "I don't know

what, but something." He rubbed my back for a little while longer. "Do you want to see what those say?"

"I'm not sure," I admitted. I'd scrunched the papers while I cried.

I straightened them now and slipped out of bed to grab a candle from the atrium. I took it back into my room and held it in one hand while I lit it.

I had that much control over my magic at least.

I held the flame over the papers and looked at the first page. It was a list of names. My mother, my father, me and five siblings. Names that, as I read them, conjured their faces in my memories. Two sisters, three brothers. Six of us in total.

"My mother's name was Alivia Talonis. My father was Terald Fineal. He was human. She was—"

"Fae," Tavian said softly. "That explains why they kept records on you in particular. Your mother was a member of the Summer Court."

"What the fuck?" I whispered. "I don't understand."

"She fell in love with a human," Tavian said slowly. "It was quite the scandal at the time. From what I gather, Cavan didn't approve. He sent them both into exile."

"And she sent me to the Temple, putting me right into his path," I said.

"It was unlikely she had a choice," Tavian said.

I screwed my eyes shut for a moment. "Right. Jezalyn, Hycanthe and I concluded they must have wiped our families' memories before taking us to the Temple. Only— is it possible to alter the memories of someone who's full Fae?"

"No," Tavian admitted. "They may have changed your father's, but they wouldn't have changed your mother's. They couldn't."

I opened my eyes. "So she was fully aware they took me. What about my other siblings?"

"I saw no other files with your second name on them," Tavian said. "It's likely you were the only omega in the family."

"Lucky me," I said sarcastically.

"Yes, lucky you. Being an omega is the best. If you weren't one, we would never have met. You wouldn't have met any of us. You would have grown up looking human, never knowing what you really are."

"I would have grown up on the farm, growing corn and all that shit," I said. "Expected to marry some nice boy from another farm or the village. Have a bunch of babies, grow old and die."

"When you put it that way, that doesn't sound so bad," he said. He took the sheets of paper from my hand and looked over the rest of them. "Just notes on how you entered the temple and when you were expected to be moved to Havenmoor." He turned to the last page.

"Confirmation none of your siblings was an omega. Or an alpha for that matter. They tested them. Here are the dates and the results."

I glanced over. Frowned. "I think that's my mother's handwriting." The flowing script triggered a memory in the back of my mind. Nothing specific, just a general sense of having seen it before.

"Why didn't they change my father's memories before he ran away with her?" I asked. "Why not have him forget her before I was even born?"

"They might have left before anyone got the chance," Tavian reasoned. "Or they weren't doing things like that back then. They might have learned their lesson from that and started doing it afterwards."

"Maybe they didn't care," I said. "Maybe they just wanted my parents to be happy."

"That's possible," Tavian agreed. "Cavan might have seen how in love they were and decided to let them be together as long as they weren't in the Summer Court. He might not be a complete asshole after all."

I wanted to cling onto that theory. Not because I gave a shit whether Cavan was an asshole or not, but because I wanted my parents to be happy. I had to believe they were. That they gave me to the Temple for my own safety, because they loved me. Because they wanted what was best for me.

"How have you heard of my mother?" I asked.

"Like I said, it was a scandal. Fae and humans fucking isn't new, but a member of the Summer Court falling in love with one is a different story. Especially when she was supposed to be betrothed to Cavan."

I blinked a couple of times. "My mother was supposed to marry Cavan?"

"I believe their parents arranged it," Tavian said. "It might have been a relief to Cavan when she chose someone else. Although, he hasn't married yet. That was only about twenty years ago though. Practically yesterday by Fae standards."

"Either way, he let her leave with the man she loved," I said. Either Cavan really didn't want to marry her, or he loved her enough to let her go. That didn't seem like the act of a complete asshole to me.

"We could lie here all night and guess," Tavian said. He put the pages aside and blew out the candle. "Or we could make the most of the time we have. Are you ready to leave yet?"

I briefly told him about my magic and Hycanthe's. He laughed at Jezalyn's suggestion that we might have problems with authority figures.

"Me too, sweetheart, me too. I'm not gonna say I'm happy about you staying here longer, but I still want to make the most of our time." He slid a hand down my side and grabbed my ass.

"Does Ryze know you're here?" I asked.

"No. I'll tell him when I get back." He rolled me onto my back and knelt between my thighs. "I'm going to need you to be very, very quiet. Can you be a good girl and not scream when I make you come?"

6

KHALA

His words sent white hot heat through me.

"What will you do if I can't?" I teased. I could, of course, I just wanted to know what he'd say.

He hummed softly. "Then I'll have to do this." He pulled something out of his pocket and pressed it between my lips. A strip of fabric. He lifted my head and tied it in place. "There, now you can't make a sound. Just in case."

He pulled something out of his other pocket, grabbed my wrists in one hand and started to tie a length of rope around them. He bound them firmly, but not too tight.

The other end of the rope, he tied to the headboard.

"Perfect," he whispered in my ear. "Now I can do whatever I want to you."

He started by sliding up the hem of my shirt until my breasts were exposed in the starlight.

"Also perfect." He swiped his tongue across one nipple, then the other. Feather light, but enough to make me shiver.

If he was anyone else but Tavian, I might not have agreed to give up control. I trusted him. He'd give me what I needed. What we both needed.

He brought a nipple between his lips and started to suck. He grazed his teeth over the sensitive peaks. Only the fabric in my mouth stopped me from moaning out loud. Instead, I moaned in the back of my throat, then panted out my nose.

"That sound was hot," he said with his mouth full of nipple. "I forgot you couldn't talk for all those years. You made up for it by making different noises. I like it. I might have to stop you from talking more often. Maybe another choker with amethyst hanging from it."

It was too dark for him to see my glare, so I growled softly instead. If anyone tried to put one of those on me again, I would tear them a new one.

He chuckled. "That sounds like agreement to me." He moved to the other nipple, lavishing attention on it before kissing his way down my stomach. He undid my pants and yanked them and my panties off in one, swift motion.

Then his face was between my thighs and he was lapping at my clit and entrance.

I was well aware someone could walk in and find us, but the only sounds I heard came from outside the slightly open window next to the bed. The ocean, shouts, the occasional passing wagon. The whisper of the wind.

We could have been alone in the whole palace. Even his mouth and my pussy were silent.

I closed my eyes and savoured the feel of his fingers sliding into my wet heat. He massaged me inside and out, until all I could do was roll my hips and buck against him.

He broke the silence only to say, "Come for me like a good girl."

I couldn't stop myself. Almost like he issued an alpha-order, I came.

I bit down on the gag and groaned into it, shattering into a million pieces before coming back together again.

"Good girl," he whispered. He lifted his shining face from me and kissed his way up the inside of my thighs.

He crawled up beside me, rolled me over onto my stomach. He pried my legs apart with his hands and knelt between them. He slipped his hand between us to position his erection, then slid inside me with almost painful slowness.

I wanted to feel him buried inside me, but he took his time, easing in bit by bit until he was fully seated to his balls.

He started to thrust, slowly at first.

"Sweetheart, you're more than worth almost getting caught and executed for."

I glanced at him over my shoulder, but that only made him laugh again. I was starting to think he might be a little crazy or maybe he had a death wish. Hopefully neither of those were contagious or an omega personality trait.

I closed my eyes and enjoyed the feeling of him sliding in and out of me. The sweet, wet friction, the feeling of being filled to the brim. Those were things I'd never get enough of.

He leaned forward and whispered, "Do you want me to come for you, sweetheart?"

I could only give him a muffled murmur as my response, along with a nod. I wanted to hear him groan as he lost himself the way I had only a few minutes earlier. The way I was about to again.

He kissed my temple. "Good, because I'm going to come inside you. I'm going to fill you up so much you overflow."

Those were the words that drove me over the edge

a second time. I pressed my face into the mattress and bucked and groaned as my whole world exploded into sprinkles of light and waves of pleasure. All punctuated by the sound of his soft groans as he too came, spilling himself inside me.

"Gods, gods, gods." He was all but breathless as he ground into me, his stomach pressed against my ass. He let out a long, last groan and slumped over me, panting, his sweated skin sliding against mine.

"Totally worth every moment."

He lay there for a while before sliding himself out of me and flopping down next to me on the mattress.

"If we were back in Lysarial, I'd leave you like that," he whispered. "I could have fun with you later or one of the others could when they happened to find you. But it's too risky here."

The idea of Ryze, Zared or Vayne walking into my room and finding me tied up, climbing on top of me and fucking me, made me warm all over again.

The idea of anyone else walking in and doing the same, was a bucket of ice cold water on my body. I didn't want to be that kind of vulnerable in a place like this.

Tavian untied my hands, then slipped the gag off my head. He shoved them both back into his pockets.

"For later. When we're both out of here."

I swallowed to get some moisture back into my

mouth. "I can't wait. It shouldn't be long. Just few days. I haven't even started to figure out what Cavan wants with my sisters. Maybe I should stay for longer, until I do."

"The longer you're here, the less I like it," Tavian said. "I still might punch Ryze for letting you come here in the first place. He should have opened a portal and sent you and Zared back to Lysarial."

"Do you think we would have gone?" Thinking about Zared made me sad all over again. I couldn't afford to get lost in that right now. I had a job to do. No matter how much I cared about him, if we didn't figure this out, thousands may die. That was what I had to concentrate on now. That and getting my sisters out. The rest, I'd deal with later.

"Probably not," Tavian agreed. He pulled up his pants and fastened them.

I hunted around for mine and slipped them back on. "You think my mother still has family in the Summer Court?" I asked.

"Considering how long Fae live, it's highly likely," he said. "Why? Do you want a family reunion with them?"

I thought about that for a few moments. "If they didn't know I existed, it was because my mother didn't want them to. If they did know about me, none of them came to stop me from going to the Temple. None of them came to tell me what I was. Not that I remember anyway. I'd like to know where I came from, but..."

"That sounds like a 'fuck them' to me," Tavian said.

I snorted. "I guess it is. For now. A day may come when I want to know them. In the meantime, I can only imagine they endorse whatever Cavan is up to. That makes them the enemy. Potentially."

"Enemy until proved friend," Tavian said. "Sometimes that's the safest way to be when it comes to Fae. Otherwise you will wake up one morning with a sword through your heart."

"That doesn't sound like you'd wake up at all to me," I said. I remembered the fish, but for some reason I couldn't bring myself to tell him. I didn't know why. I trusted him, but something like that was— I don't know. The fewer people who knew about it the better. It seemed to me like a dangerous skill to have.

Of course, I was guessing about all of this. For all I knew, Dalyth brought people back from the dead on a daily basis. Or one of the other omegas. Or another Fae who could use magic.

I wanted to ask about it, but I didn't. I'd save those questions for Ryze.

"Good point," Tavian said. "You certainly wouldn't. Unless you count waking up in one of the hells. Since people only guess what they're like, then who knows?"

"What do Fae think the hells are like?" I asked. In

spite of worshiping, or pretending to worship, the gods, the priests and priestesses went into very little detail about what the hells entailed. Not much beyond 'you don't want to end up there.' Their ideal was to spend eternity on the palm of one of the gods.

I'd never given much thought as to what that actually meant. Presumably some poor deity couldn't close their hand because it was covered in souls.

"Eternity in a room full of strangers who don't like you for no apparent reason, no comfortable beds and no cake," he replied.

"Is that the Fae version of the hells, or yours?" I asked teasingly.

"Definitely mine," he said. "Although, in mine, you're not there either. Now I want to eat cake off your body. Can we do that when we get back home?"

"Sure," I said, although I wasn't sure if Lysarial was home. I didn't know where home was right now. How could I go back there and live my life without Zared? Without ever seeing him or hearing his voice? Without seeing him get angry, or watching him watch me crawl to him.

"I'm sorry I didn't try harder to get both of you back to the Winter Court," Tavian said. "I should throw you over my shoulder right now and get you out of here. Your sisters sound like they can take care of themselves."

"I'm not going yet," I said steadily. "There's more at stake than just me. But you should go. The sun will rise soon. If you're found here..."

He glanced at the window. "Fuck. You're right. I'd hide under your bed, but Ryze is going to want an update. You know what he's like."

I did know. Ryze would want every detail.

Tavian rolled over and kissed me. "I'll be back tonight, if I can. And the night after that. And every night until I can take you out of here."

"Don't put yourself at risk unless you have to," I said. "I'm fine here." More or less.

"If you've felt how your pussy feels around my cock, you'd know I have to," he said. "Besides which, it's my job as one of your packmates to keep you safe and I can't do that if I don't check up on you."

There was clearly no arguing with him, so I sighed softly. "Be careful, all right?"

"I'm always careful," he said, cocky as ever. "That's what makes me so good at what I do. I know how to avoid getting caught."

Those sounded like famous last words to me, but I hoped he was right. I didn't want to lose him too. Even though I wasn't exactly sure where home was right now, my attachment to him went beyond the bond. I was sure he felt the same way too. He hadn't *just* snuck into fuck me, he was here because he cared. Because he couldn't stay away.

And so he could fuck me.

"Will you tell Ryze about my mother?" I asked.

"Do you want me to?" He ran the pad of his thumb down my cheek.

"I think I'd rather tell him myself," I said slowly. If he was going to be angry about my connection to Cavan and the Summer Court, I wanted to see that on his face. I didn't want him to have enough time to compose himself and the perfect answer if he decided to reject me. He said he wouldn't lie to me again, but that didn't mean he wouldn't think up some half-truths to save my feelings or whatever his intention might be.

"I'll keep it to myself then," Tavian said. "It won't be long until you can tell him to his face. And Vayne."

It was too dark for him to see my grimace. I hadn't thought about telling Vayne. No doubt he'd be very forthcoming with his thoughts.

"Until later." Tavian gave me a long, lingering kiss on the mouth. Only the dipping of the bed indicated that he'd stood and slipped away, leaving me alone in the last hour of darkness before another sunrise.

7

TAVIAN

"You went fucking *where?*" Ryze snarled.

"To the Summer Palace to check on Khala," I repeated. "If you're worried about it, I did the rounds with my contacts first. They didn't have much to—"

"I don't give a shit about your contacts." He stalked away a few steps, then whirled around to face me. "You shouldn't have gone anywhere near the palace. In case you forgot, none of us are supposed to be in the city. If you were caught, there would have been repercussions for all of us. Including Khala. Do you think she'd last five minutes past them finding out we orchestrated them taking her? That, in spite of telling me to leave because she wanted to know about her parents, she's still working with us."

"She's still working with us?" Vayne asked. He

shook his head, visibly confused and more than slightly frustrated.

"Of course she is," I replied easily. "This is a chance for her to learn about herself and her magic, but she's still ours. She hasn't found out what Cavan wants with the omegas yet. Hopefully soon."

That was the easy part out of the way. Now for the hard part.

I took a moment, then told them about Zared.

"Shit," Ryze said softly. "That wasn't supposed to happen. We had someone in place—"

"They weren't able to act quickly enough," I said. "Thank the gods they didn't kill him."

"That was a very real, potential possibility," Ryze said. "They both knew that. Zared was willing to take the risk for her."

"Yes, and look where that got him." I flopped down into a chair. "It was a calculated risk, but that doesn't make it suck any less."

"No, it doesn't," Ryze agreed. "How is she doing? Honestly. Is she all right?" He looked as though he might open a portal then and there to go and get her. Only the fact he'd never been to the atrium stopped him. There wasn't anywhere he could portal to that wouldn't be full of Summer Court guards. He'd kill his way through if he had to, but that was a last resort.

"She was fine when I left her." I couldn't help looking smug.

"You fucking didn't," Vayne said, scowling at me. "Bad enough that you went there at all. I can almost commend you for sneaking in to check on her, but going in to fuck her?"

"Would you believe it just happened?" I asked.

"No," they both said together.

"We know you too well for that," Ryze said with a half smile. His annoyance wasn't completely gone, but it had cooled.

"Disappointed I didn't stick around to fuck you?" I teased.

His only response was to raise an eyebrow. He wasn't given to overt displays of affection or deep and meaningful conversations about personal emotions. Some days that left me not knowing where I stood with him. I knew he cared about me. It went beyond the occasional fuck, but I didn't know how far beyond. He was so busy being High Lord, it wouldn't surprise me if he didn't take the time to think about it. Whatever happened, happened and he rolled with it.

And me, I tried not to be pushy. With Khala in the picture, things were even more complicated, but in the best way. Like sugar in a cup of tea. Or the pleading look in someone's eye before I cut their throat.

"How much longer is she going to be in there?"

Vayne asked.

"Not much longer." I broke eye contact with Ryze and turned to Vayne.

I told them what little I could, that I hadn't told them already.

"I don't like her being there," Ryze said. "I don't like either of you being in there. Hells, I don't like being there either. Cavan is a fucking snake."

"So is Harel," Wornar said from where he stood, leaning against the wall. His legs were crossed at his ankles, arms crossed over his chest.

He was handsome, but there was something about him I could never quite trust. I wasn't sure what, just something not right. I didn't turn my back on anyone but Ryze, Vayne, Zared and Khala, but him... I always had an extra half an eye on him.

"Now we've confirmed they're working together, I should get back to the Spring Court and let Thiron know." Wornar remained leaning against the wall.

"Knowing Thiron, he'd want more information than that," Ryze said. "What the fuck they're up to, for a start. Stick around. I have a feeling things are about to get interesting."

"Interesting in a way that might end up with us dead, or interesting in an entertaining way?" Wornar asked. "Because I know which one I'm interested in. I'd prefer not to end up dead."

"We figured that was the one you meant," Ryze told him. "As long as I've known you, you've never had a death wish. If you want to scurry back to the Spring Court, go ahead, but you know I'm right about Thiron. He'll want details."

Wornar uncrossed his legs and grimaced. "I hate to admit that you're right, but he would. What are we going to do about it then? The direct approach got us nowhere."

"Now it's time for the sneaky as fuck approach," Ryze said. "Which, incidentally, is one of my favourite approaches."

"Funny, mine too," I said. The shadows were one of my favourite places to be. Apart from snuggled in my nest, with someone I cared about around my cock. Or me around theirs. Priorities.

"You're definitely going to get me killed one of these days," Wornar said.

"I keep telling them the same thing," Vayne said. "Sometimes I think they have a bet going on about who they can get killed and how quickly. So far, we've both defied the odds. At some point, our luck is going to run out."

"That's what I'm afraid of," Wornar said, the side of his mouth pulled back.

"Isn't it better to die having a good time than live for a long time bored out of your mind?" Ryze asked.

"I'd rather have fun *and* a long life," Vayne said with a grunt.

"And yet, you became a soldier," I pointed out.

"I know." Vayne sighed. "I should have gone into my family business, making pots and vases for rich Fae."

I closed my eyes and pretended to snore loudly. When I opened them again, it was to see Vayne give me a rude gesture with his middle finger.

I grinned.

"Admit it, you'd be bored out of your mind," I told him. "You'd take up pot throwing, just for something to do."

"I might take that up anyway. Care to be my target?"

"Thank you, but I think I'll pass," I said. "Can I suggest you keep it in mind if we go to war? A pot throwing regiment could be fun."

"We do that anyway," Vayne pointed out. "Pots of hot oil."

I snapped my fingers. "That's right. I knew it was a good idea."

Vayne rolled his eyes at me.

"Are they always like this?" Wornar asked Ryze.

"Always." Ryze nodded. "I'm starting to suspect they were both born backwards. Or dropped on their heads as infants."

"That would explain why we spend so much time with you," Vayne told him.

"I thought that was because I paid you." Ryze cocked his head at Vayne.

"That too," Vayne agreed. "Otherwise, I'd be out of here."

"It's a long walk home," I remarked. "If you started now, we'd get there before you."

"As entertaining as this is," Wornar started, "it doesn't address the question of what we're going to do. Ryze, you mentioned something about being sneaky as fuck?"

"I did, didn't I? I was thinking we could sneak into the Summer Court barracks. See if they're mobilising, or training for anything in particular. Like walking on ice. Melting ice. What to do in a sudden snowstorm."

"In other words, ways to attack the Winter Court," I said.

"Precisely," Ryze agreed.

"And if they're coming after us?" Wornar asked. "I hate to admit it, but Spring Court magic isn't as dramatic. They wouldn't need to plan for any special conditions."

"That's true, but if they're training more soldiers than usual, we'll know they're up to something, even if we don't know what." Ryze tapped his finger on his lip.

"Tave, have you got people we can send in if that's the case? If Cavan and Harel's aim is a full on attack, they aren't going to turn anyone away, or ask too many questions."

"I see what I can organise," I said with a nod. "We have one or two people here in Garial who might be suitable. Assuming they're both sober, that is."

I couldn't guarantee anything when it came to the people I worked with. They wouldn't work with me if they weren't dubious characters to begin with.

Ryze nodded. "Good enough. I'd be happier if we had more ears in the palace, but it is what it is. Let's go check out the barracks."

"Now?" Vayne stared at him. "In broad daylight?"

"They won't be expecting us to turn up there, especially during the day," Ryze said. "In case we're noticed, both of you stick to Wornar or me. We'll be able to make a quick portal and get the fuck out of there."

Vayne closed his eyes and shook his head. "This isn't even the stupidest idea you've had this week." In spite of that, he picked up his sword from where it leaned against the wall and slid it into the sheath on his back.

"Thank you," Ryze told him. "I think."

Vayne responded with an eloquent roll of his eyes. Which was funny, because I knew he enjoyed all of this as much as the rest of us did. Sometimes, I thought he just enjoyed being grumpy.

Why, I had no idea.

8

TAVIAN

alking like we belonged in the city, we wound our way through the streets of Garial. Most people didn't give us a second glance. The only ones who did, made eyes at Ryze and Wornar. That was understandable. They were both attractive men, both oozing power, in magic and in authority. A heady combination for sure.

I walked a little behind the others. It was my job to be inconspicuous. Walking with them was anything but. Three men walking through the city might go unnoticed, but four? Much less likely.

In addition, the moment someone started to follow them, I noticed. She was also trying to be inconspicuous, but I could spot someone or something suspicious out of a crowd faster than most.

When she stopped at a stand on the side of the

street to admire a belt, I stopped at another stand to look at a knife.

It was well made and well-balanced. If I needed another knife, I would have bought it. I made a mental note to come back later.

When the woman moved on from the belt stand, I put down the knife, smiled at the blacksmith and walked on slowly through the crowds.

She wound her way through, stopping every so often, but always keeping Ryze and the others in sight. She even bought a small cake from one of the stands and ate it as she followed. It looked so good, I bought one myself. Then one each for the others. No doubt they'd appreciate the treat later.

Unless I got hungry and ate them first.

Now, where was the woman? I glanced around surreptitiously before casually opening the bag and pulling out a cake.

I was halfway through eating it when she stepped out of an alley, right in front of me and put a knife to my throat.

"Why are you following me?" she rasped.

I looked down at the blade, then went on eating. "The question is, what are you doing in Garial, Illaria? You're a long way from the Winter Court."

"I could ask you the same thing, Master Tavian," she said.

"You could, but it's none of your business," I replied. I'd seen her plenty of times around the palace. Usually watching Fae men without shirts sparring in the practice ring. Her bright red hair and emerald green eyes were difficult to miss. Especially in the Winter Court.

I pushed the knife away from my throat with my wrist and finished the last of my cake.

"You didn't answer my question. What is a woman who looks like she's straight out of the Autumn Court, who lives in the *Winter* Court, doing here in the *Summer* Court? If you ask me, all of that is very suspicious. Added to that, you were following Ryzellius. Don't tell me you didn't notice him walking right in front of you."

She didn't flinch, but she put away her blade. Lucky for her, because if she tried to use it, she'd be dead in a heartbeat. And then Ryze would be pissed I made a mess in the street.

"I might have noticed," she said noncommittally. "I also have it on good authority Cavan ordered him out of the city. Before you say it, half the city is talking about it."

I doubted it was anything like that much, but I wouldn't call her out on it. People did like to gossip, and often didn't care what they were gossiping about. When you were a spymaster or a Master of Assassins, you tended to listen to it. On occasion, some of it was even true.

"We're starting to attract attention." I nodded for her to step back into the alley. "Now, you have approximately a minute to explain what you're doing here. Otherwise, the next set of bones drying here will be yours."

She looked huffy. "I was sent here."

"By whom?" I asked. "Not by me. Not by Ryze or Vayne either. Let me guess, direct order from Harel?"

"Fuck no," she said quickly. She actually looked disgusted at the idea. "There's a faction in the Autumn Court who are concerned about what he's doing here. They sent me to find out."

"You work for a faction that wants to rival the High Lord of the Autumn Court," I said slowly. "Why do you live in the Winter Court?"

She shrugged. "I like it."

I cocked my head at her.

She sighed. "Fine, I'm in exile from the Autumn Court. That faction, they, *we*, made a move against him a few years ago. We weren't successful, obviously. He had a lot of them executed, but some of us got out first. Now we can't go back. We'll be killed on sight."

I frowned. "Why have I not heard of any of this?" It was my job to know things like this. If I didn't know, then spymaster Bravenna didn't know either. This kind of information would have reached my ears if it reached Ryze's.

"It was all done quietly, including the executions," Illaria said. "Harel has been trying to increase his power for a long time now. His influence too. We believe he's here to do just that."

"We could have saved you the trouble of coming here," I said. "We think the same thing." I wasn't concerned about telling her that, since she clearly knew plenty already.

She almost looked sulky as she said, "I didn't know you knew. Those I work with, we're few and we're vulnerable. We have influence of our own, but Harel is aware of us. We speculated whether or not we could align ourselves with any of the other courts, but we didn't know who we could trust. We still don't."

"I think it's more or less fair to say, at this point, any enemy of Harel is a friend of ours," I said. "Any enemy of Cavan too, for that matter."

"Including Khala?" Illaria asked. "I saw her being taken to the palace. Shame, she seemed so nice. And her human friend too."

When I didn't say anything, she continued, "You're trying to get her out, aren't you? I can help."

"How?" I asked. "You can't even follow people down the street without being detected."

"You need to give yourself more credit," she told me.

"No one else would have noticed me but you. You wouldn't be a very good Master of Assassins otherwise."

"That might be true," I said. "Or you might have been more obvious than you thought." I admit to getting a touch of sadistic pleasure at the look of discomfort on her face. I got it, no one liked to have their skills questioned.

On the other hand, I didn't trust anyone who tried to butter me up. She might have told the truth about a secret faction who plotted against Harel, and she might have been lying through her teeth. It seemed much more likely that she worked for Harel and was trying to keep an eye on us. If that was the case, he needed to hire some better spies.

"Are we going to stand here talking all day, or are we going to do whatever it is you're supposed to be doing right now?" she asked.

"Who says I'm not supposed to be doing exactly this?" I opened the bag of cakes and pulled out the one intended for Vayne.

"No one makes cake quite like the bakers in the Summer Court." That was a lie. It was all right, but not anywhere near as nice as what we got back home. Whatever, I was hungry.

"Basic logic says so," she retorted. "You were following them, watching out for anyone else who was also following them. And now you're not following them, so if anyone is, you're not there to see it."

I took a bite out of Vayne's cake, then dropped it back in the bag and folded down the top.

"That's true, you sidetracked me by following them," I told her. "But trust me when I say they can take care of themselves. The worst thing that'll happen right now is them missing out on cake."

The worst thing that could happen would be them being caught and killed, but missing cake was pretty high on the list of bad things to happen. Even if it was only mediocre cake.

"Are we going to catch up to them?" she asked. "We can't be that far behind."

"I'm going to keep going," I said. I stood here long enough. My skin started to twitch with impatience. That wasn't a good thing for anyone.

"I'm going with you," she insisted. "I have a vested interest in this too. The Autumn Court can't keep going on like it has. Harel is bleeding us dry. Families can't afford the taxes he's putting on them, and if they can't pay..."

I gestured for her to finish her sentence. The Autumn Court coffers were none of my business, unless innocent Fae were suffering. If that was the case, I might make it my business. Or Ryze's. I was almost sure he'd love something else to stick his nose into.

Okay, probably not, but I'd make it his business anyway. He could thank me later.

"Some of them have had to join the army," she said. "Others have disappeared."

I frowned. If that was the case, the Autumn Court wasn't the only one making people disappear. Several assassins sent to the Summer Court had gone missing. None of my contacts had any idea where they'd gone. Nothing beyond educated guesses. That likely being the case, I doubted we'd ever find their remains. Their family mausoleums, where the skulls of Fae were placed on stone shelves in neat lines, would forever miss having theirs there too.

"How many would have gone into the army?" I couldn't do anything for Fae who were already dead, but taking people into the army was extreme, even for the Autumn Court.

"More than necessary, given we're not at war." Her expression was grim, her green eyes troubled. I found it more and more difficult not to believe what she was saying.

Voices out on the street reminded me we shouldn't linger here too long. Nothing said 'suspicious' like two people standing in an alley, talking in low voices.

I thought quickly. "Fine, you can come with me. But

if you get in the way, or do anything that would in any way indicate I can't trust you, I will kill you."

I thought about doing it now, just to save time, and to satisfy the urge I got all too frequently. The overwhelming desire to feel warm blood on my hand and see the light fade from their eyes. Did Ryze feel that powerful when he used magic? Surely there couldn't be anything more powerful than taking a life.

"I could say the same to you," she said. "I guess we're going to have to trust each other."

I made a slight noise of agreement in the back of my throat. "Try not to get in my way." After a moment I added, "And never put a knife to my throat again. That's the quickest way for you to end up dead."

"Don't give me a reason," she retorted.

I won't lie, my hand twitched near one of my knives. Not because I planned to kill her, but I was curious to see her response if I looked like I was going to.

I held the bag of cakes at my side and gestured towards the street. "Let's go then. We'll need to hurry a bit to catch up. Without looking like we're hurrying."

I didn't wait to see if she understood what I meant. I stepped back out onto the street and wove through the crowds. They seemed thicker now.

I walked faster than I had before, but still meandered, stopping here and there to look at stands, and to give way to wagons that crossed sidestreets.

Nothing more than a good citizen of Garial.

In the corner of my eye, I saw her catch up to me. I made a note to give her some lessons in stealth later. No wonder the uprising against Harel failed. They needed better sneaking skills.

"Where are we going?" she asked.

"North," I said. I stepped around a pair of children who sat on the side of the street, rolling marbles back and forth between them.

"No shit. Where specifically?" She glanced over at me without breaking her stride.

"Specifically north a couple of blocks from here," I said. "That's all I'm saying. If you don't want to come, then don't."

"You don't trust me," she accused.

"We don't trust each other," I agreed. "But I let you live and I'm letting you come with me. If you keep arguing, it's going to start looking suspicious."

She made a sound of annoyance, but fell quiet after that.

That left me to my thoughts, and the job of scanning the street in front of us. I saw no sign of Ryze and the others, but they couldn't be too far away. I hoped. I'd catch up with them sooner or later, but I hated the idea no one had their backs.

Yes, they could look after themselves, but it was easier this way. Easier if I could neutralise any threats before they caught up to them.

Easier if I wasn't...

I looked over to Illaria at the same time I had that thought. I saw it on her face that she knew the realisation I'd come to.

"What did you fucking do?" I hissed.

"Only what I was told to do," she said with no hint of apology. "Distract you for a while."

"Fuck." If the street wasn't so busy, I would have slid a knife between her ribs and kept going. That wouldn't go unnoticed and I had no time to waste. No time to be stealthy.

I started down the road at the fastest trot I could manage, dodging the crowds and darting in front of carriages. One almost hit me, but I managed to duck aside in time.

I was almost to the barracks when the air filled with thick, acrid smoke. Ash started to drop from the sky. When a dusting landed on my sleeve, I realised it wasn't ash.

It was snow.

9

KHALA

I expected to see Cavan at some point. When he finally sauntered into the atrium, everyone scattered. All of the omegas suddenly found somewhere else to be.

Dalyth ended another frustrating lesson and ushered Hycanthe and Jezalyn away.

They both gave me sympathetic looks, but neither hesitated to leave. The gods only knew where Dalyth was taking them, but right now there was nothing I could do to stop her. When I started to follow, she waved at me to stay.

The place was cleared in about a minute, apart from Cavan and me. He stood near the door, appraising me with his gaze. He didn't look at me like a man would look at a woman, not exactly. This was more like the way a man might look at a newly forged sword. Or the perfect bow. Appreciative but like I was a tool he owned and planned to use.

"I trust you're settling in all right." His tone was smooth like silk. He circled around me slowly, his eyes on me at every step.

"It's fine," I said simply, not moving a hair.

"Only fine?" He stopped to tilt his head. "That sounds inadequate."

I shrugged. "A girl can only see so much of the same four walls."

I wasn't necessarily trying to antagonise him, my answers were honest. I discovered the older omegas were allowed to leave the atrium. Presumably they'd proved their loyalty somehow. I wasn't sure I wanted to know what that took. Maybe they'd kept their thoughts to themselves better than I was.

"Surely this is nicer than the temple?" He resumed walking slowly.

"I was allowed outside there," I replied. "They let the maidens enjoy the fresh air."

"That sounds like a small freedom compared to the others which were withheld. The ability to speak. The choice to worship the gods, or not."

"You don't worship the gods?" I wasn't sure why I asked. Curiosity? To make conversation? Because the way he was looking at me was unnerving?

All of those things.

He stepped back around in front of me. "When you've lived a long time, you start to question many things. Including the existence of gods. Perhaps people want someone to look up to. Perhaps they want someone to blame. Perhaps the gods created us, and perhaps we created ourselves."

"Are you saying Fae are gods?" I looked over at his hooded blue eyes. I could only begin to imagine the things he'd seen in his hundreds of years of life. So many things I had yet to see. In the scheme of things, I'd just begun.

"What do you think?" he asked.

"I don't think we are," I said. "But I think some of us like to play at being gods."

I was worried I might piss him off, but he laughed.

"Me, you mean. I'm sure Dalyth has explained why you're here. The safety of you and your omega sisters was important to me. Would you prefer I left you to whatever fate you would have had amongst the humans? I don't think you would have liked it. It's certainly not as nice as this." He gestured towards the window, and the expansive view beyond.

"I'd prefer not to have seen priests killed," I replied. "Was that necessary?"

"Unfortunately, yes," he said. "I tried to negotiate with the temple, but they were...unreasonable. The choices I had were: attack the temple in Ebonfalls, the Temple in Havenmoor, or the caravan. The caravan seemed like the option which would lead to the least amount of carnage. Wouldn't you agree?"

"I suppose so," I conceded reluctantly. Fewer people were on those carriages than would have been in either temple. Still, attacking them seemed extreme.

"Dalyth couldn't have stopped the caravan and tried to talk?"

Cavan pressed his finger to his lower lip. "Before Dalyth had the role of intercepting omegas, the job went to a lovely Fae woman by the name of Jayde. She tried this approach. Since the role now falls to Dalyth, do I need to tell you what happened to Jayde?"

Before I could respond, he continued, "They were nice enough to remove her head from her shoulders neatly enough that her skull could be placed in her family's mausoleum. They weren't as kind with several Fae in her company. The three omegas who transformed from that group of Silent Maidens were buried along with them."

"I've considered the option of bringing all of those girls, the *potential* omegas, to the Summer Court, but I suspect they wouldn't care for that arrangement. The maidens seem like a more gentle approach. Although, of course, the end isn't gentle for everyone."

I hated the fact he was making so much sense. If I

was taken from my mother and brought here, I would have been even more terrified and confused than when I went to the Temple. Stepping out for fresh air in a city full of Fae might have been a death sentence. At best, I would have attracted a lot of stares.

"I see you're starting to understand," he said smoothly. "This isn't ideal, but it is for your own good. I'm sure Ryzellius has filled your head with all sorts of lies and confusion. For some reason, he seems to think we're plotting against him."

"You're not?" I asked.

"Only in as much as I intend to keep doing what's best for the omegas," he said smoothly. "I'd prefer not to let innocent young women suffer because of his oversized ego."

I managed to contain an outward response to his words, if only out of some kind of loyalty to Ryze. Loyalty I was starting to question.

"Have you told him what you're doing? Maybe he and the other High Lords would help you. They may even figure out a way to avoid any further bloodshed, or scared young women."

"I've sent messengers and envoys. Either the High Lords won't listen or the envoys don't return at all. After a few attempts, it seemed fruitless to keep trying." He sighed heavily.

I frowned. From what I'd seen of Harel, I could

totally imagine him ignoring Cavan. But not Ryze. And not the Spring Court if Wornar was any indication.

"Harel is working with you," I said finally.

"The only reasonable one," Cavan said sadly. "Ironic given his...usually unreasonable behaviour."

"What does he want in return?" I asked. "Some omegas of his own?"

"Probably," Cavan agreed. "Once you're trained in the use of your magic, you're welcome to make that choice for yourself."

"Really?" I asked cautiously. "You'd let me leave the Summer Court?"

"You're not a prisoner here, Khala. You're here for your own protection. Once you're ready, your life is your own."

"If I decide to go back to the Winter Court, you won't stop me?"

"I'd be surprised if you want to go back after learning what you've learnt already, much less what you'll learn in the following months. However, if that's what you want, I won't stop you." He spread his hands.

"What do you tell the maidens when they first arrive here?" I clasped my hand in front of me and levelled my gaze at him.

His brows dipped. "We tell them the truth. It's difficult for them to accept, but those who transition deserve to know there's a possibility. Those who don't, won't remember it later." He hesitated, then drew his head back slightly, chin raised. "Ryzellius didn't tell you, did he? He left you to find out for yourself."

I couldn't help the renewed bubble of anger that boiled inside me. I didn't want to think too badly of Ryze, but he *had* kept all of that from me.

"He told me the heat would happen," I said slowly.

"But that's all," Cavan stated. "He didn't tell you you may transition?"

"Because he wasn't sure I would." I felt the need to defend him, at least a little. "He didn't want to scare me." It sounded weak, even to myself.

"Winter Court magic can't change memories," Cavan said. "Anything he told you, you would have remembered and he knew it. And so he took away your right to know what was going to happen. He lied to you."

My lips moved, but no sound came out. I couldn't deny a word. I presumed what he said about Winter Court magic was true. He'd know more about that than I would. Although, wouldn't Ryze know someone who could change my memories if he wanted it done? But he hadn't, he flat out lied instead.

"I can see from the expression on your face that was precisely what occurred," Cavan said.

I didn't feel him take my hand, but there it was with both of his clasped around it. "You don't owe him anything."

Where our skin touched, mine tingled. It wasn't attraction, I told myself. It was an alpha-omega instinctive reaction. My body wanted to curl into his, to seek his warmth and protection. To obey.

I forced myself to slip my hand away, and tucked them under my arms.

"I'm sure he didn't mean any harm."

Cavan barked a short laugh. If he was annoyed at me for drawing away, he didn't show it.

"I'm sure he didn't mean any harm to *himself*. I very much doubt he gave a shit about you. Did he tell you he did?"

"He might have," I said evasively. Those were personal conversations I wanted to keep to myself. That and the mating bond. He didn't need to know about that connection.

"I can see you're conflicted," Cavan said. "You may not wish to take up this offer, but I can ask Dalyth to put him out of your mind, so to speak."

"No," I said immediately. "Thank you. I'd rather... deal with everything and move on when I'm ready. I don't want to forget anything." No matter how fucked up it was. Or how fucked up it *might* be. Honestly, I wasn't sure who to believe right now. Who to trust.

"Ryze believes what you're doing here is messing with the weather." I might as well get an answer to that, if Cavan would give me one.

He sighed. "Unfortunately, he's right on that count. In a manner of speaking. You will have noticed it gets hotter in here after you've been practising for a while. There are dozens of omegas learning to use Summer Court magic and Fae teaching them. Here and in other parts of the court. We've noticed the more that happens, the more it impacts the temperature here and in the rest of Jorius. We've been trying to find a way to contain it, but we haven't been successful yet. As you might imagine, some of my advisers have suggested they stop practising. Some have insisted we dispose of those omegas."

He let the words hang in the air for a moment.

"I don't agree with either of those options. Thus, we're still looking for a solution. If you think of one, please let me or Dalyth know. Endless summer would be tiresome, even for the Lord of Summer."

That made too much sense too. We noticed how hot the atrium was after lessons. Every time we were done, I'd cool it down. I told him that.

He looked thoughtful. "That might be something we can try. It can't hurt."

With any luck, it wouldn't. Magic seemed a lot more complicated than anyone let on.

He regarded me for a long moment before he spoke again. "I'm not what you expected, am I?"

10

———

KHALA

"**A**ren't you?" I asked back. "What was I expecting?"

"Knowing Ryzellius, a power hungry asshole. Which is relatively accurate. But no more than he is. No more than any other High Lord. Most of us inherit the role, but there are always those who seek to take it from us. If the Fae are good at anything, it's biding our time. There are plots which will have been bubbling for decades. Centuries. Sometimes planning, sometimes just passing the time. Boredom can be a side effect of living so long. Some have nothing else to do but plot in the shadows. Once in a while, they'll appear and act. It makes things interesting for a while. Then they disappear again. Back into hiding, or defeated."

"Sometimes it results in war," I said. Ryze had remarked multiple times that all he wanted to do was avoid that happening again. He seemed so sure Cavan was pushing in that direction. Or maybe he just wanted me to think that.

"Sometimes war is inevitable," Cavan said.

"Nothing is inevitable," I said.

"It might seem that way when you're as young as you are. When too many times you've seen conflict escalate until all that's left is to pick up a sword and use it." He clearly spoke from experience.

"Sometimes you have to pick up a sword to defend yourself." I couldn't imagine arming myself to go on the attack. To protect me and my sisters, I would, without hesitation. And my pack? I wasn't even sure that was real anymore. If Cavan's plan was to seed doubt in my mind, he succeeded. My brain swirled with them.

"I'll always defend myself," he said. "No matter who comes after me and what's mine."

The words echoed between us for a moment.

"You know I was supposed to marry your mother." His words broke the silence.

I tried to keep the surprise off my face but failed. How did he know I knew? Or was he just guessing?

"You were?" I said carefully.

From the look on his face, he knew not only that I knew, but how.

"You look like her. Your hair is a bit lighter. Eyes a

bit darker. Your nose is the same." He cocked his head. "Same forthright personality. People didn't fuck with her either. Once Alivia made up her mind about something, there was no changing it. All she wanted was Terald."

His lip curled slightly.

"If she didn't, I wouldn't exist," I pointed out.

He seemed amused at that. "You still would, but you would have been mine instead." After a beat, he added, "In a different way to the way you are now."

He brushed his knuckles over my cheek. The touch was light, but it was enough to trigger that instinctual alpha-omega connection. That tiny burst of need. Did he feel it too?

I drew my face back. I didn't want an added layer of confusion on top of everything else.

"Did you want to be with her?" I asked.

He lowered his hand to his side, then softly said, "Very much. I would have killed Terald to keep her, but she stood between us. Literally. I would have had to kill her to get to him. I exiled them instead. That's one reason I don't like humans in the Summer Court. I'm a bitter, vindictive asshole."

He smiled slightly. "I wouldn't have hesitated to kill that friend of yours if I didn't think it would put you off side. If you weren't Alivia's daughter, I wouldn't have even cared about that."

"Can you build bridges with Summer Court magic?" I asked dryly. "Because it sounds like you need to build one and get over it."

He looked surprised, then laughed. "That's probably likely. You're the first person in twenty years to say anything like that to my face. The first since Alivia. No one else would dare."

"I hear it's not healthy to surround yourself with people who won't tell you what they think," I said. "You start to believe everything you do is right."

"You might be correct," he said. "Although, everything I do *is* right. And if it isn't, I'm sure you'll tell me." The side of his mouth twitched upward.

"If I stay here," I reminded him. "I might leave and travel around the courts. Find a nice cottage in a forest or beside a beach. Live a quiet life by myself."

"You're an omega," he reminded me, as if I could possibly forget. "It's not your fate to spend your existence alone. You're meant to be taken care of, treasured. Which, in turn, is what alphas are for. To cater to your every need and whim. To bring you the stars when you ask for them. To saddle the moon."

"What would I do with the stars and the moon?" I scoffed.

"Whatever you want," he said. "But you don't need either of those. They're already in your eyes."

I snorted. "That's very...poetic. Did you say the same thing to my mother?"

He actually flinched minutely. "I might have. It didn't work on her either."

He had the grace to look sheepish. He was right, he wasn't what I expected. I couldn't decide if he was sweet or way too good to be true. Or just a good actor.

I couldn't, wouldn't, dismiss everything Ryze, Vayne and Tavian told me about him, based on one conversation. In the end, he still had Zared sent back to Ebonfalls. I had no real reason to trust him. I was basically a prisoner here.

"If it's my whim, can I go and get some air?" I gave him a challenging look.

Predictably, he responded with a sigh and a shake of his head.

Before he could speak, I said, "Let me guess. For my own protection, I have to stay here."

"I heard you froze my fish." He glanced down at the reflecting pool.

"I heard they usually get boiled," I retorted.

"I really need to stop restocking that pool," he said. "It looks so much nicer with fish swimming around in there. The alternative is to keep the omegas in the dungeon, and I suspect that wouldn't be well received."

"Nothing says 'prisoner' like putting someone in a dungeon," I agreed. "At least this cage is pretty."

He looked at me like he wanted to say something, but forced his gaze over to the window.

"Yes it is. Best view in all of Garial. Sometimes I think we're justified in changing the maiden's memories because no one would want to leave this and go to Havenmoor."

"You've been to Havenmoor?"

"A long time ago," he said vaguely. "I remember old stone buildings and new timber ones. An old well and lots of mud. Nothing to compare to Fae cities."

When he put it that way, he had a point. Not that a gilded cage was preferable to anything, including mud, but if he meant what he said about letting me go, then Garial or Lysarial were nicer places to be than anywhere I'd seen in Fraxius.

That speculation was all moot anyway, since I couldn't go back and live in Fraxius with a Fae face. Either way, I'd end up somewhere in Jorius.

"Is that why the Fae moved out of Fraxius?" I asked. "To get away from all the mud?"

"I don't know why," he admitted. "That could have been it. Plenty of us don't like getting our hands and feet dirty."

He was smiling again. I wasn't sure if he was joking or not.

"Poor babies," I said sarcastically. "My mother wasn't afraid of getting her hands dirty."

"No she wasn't," he agreed. "Or bloody. I'm guessing she didn't tell you she was a soldier."

I shook my head at him in disbelief. "My mother? Are you sure we're talking about the same woman? She didn't even tell me she was Fae. I don't remember ever seeing her ears." I lightly touched my own with my fingertips.

"You wouldn't have." He closed his eyes tightly. "She was so determined to fit in, she had them changed. The woman did such a terrible job on her, I had her executed. Thank the gods Alivia had slightly human-shaped eyes. I'd hate to think what she would have done to herself if she hadn't."

I thought back again to that memory. To the sense that I knew she said something about having an accident. But she'd done it on purpose, because she loved my father that much.

"I'm starting to think it would have been safer if she and my father stayed in Jorius," I said. I didn't bother to keep the accusation out of my tone. If he sent them away and made her so desperate she let herself be mutilated, then he should wear some of the blame for that.

"Possibly," he conceded. "Those were the choices made then. They cannot be unmade. All we can do is learn from the shit we did in the past and move on.

Build the bridge, as you so eloquently said, and get over it."

"If you knew what she'd do, would you have let them stay?" I asked.

He stepped over to the window and leaned his forehead against the glass. "If I let them stay, different mistakes would have been made. By me or by... someone else." He shook his head. His breath misted the window, before evaporating again. His regret seemed genuine.

"I can't guarantee you would have been born if they'd stayed. I have no idea what would have happened. Summer Court magic doesn't allow us to see alternative presents. Or futures, for that matter."

"Do any court magics allow that?" The ability to see the future would be a useful skill to have.

"Only one and it's probably a myth." He looked over at me, gazing under long lashes. "According to legend, there are two more courts."

Without thinking I said, "The Court of Shadows and the Court of Dreams." Should have I told him I'd heard of those? The words had left my lips. It was too late to take them back.

He didn't look surprised. "According to the legends, Fae in the Court Of Dreams could see the future. They saw their own demise, and instead of letting it take them, they disappeared. Some said they planned to be gone for a thousand years."

"And the Court of Shadows?"

He turned around and leaned his back against the window. "Just like the seasonal courts, they had their opposite. The Court of Shadows and the Court of Dreams. They say those in the shadows could see the past. Lives and civilisations that are now long gone. According to legend, both courts were bitter enemies. Shadows wanted to destroy the Court of Dreams. They say if they are found again, they will destroy each other and all of Jorius."

He stopped for a moment and looked contemplative, like he wasn't sure if he should tell me more.

Finally, he continued, "I believe both courts exist. There's been conflict and strange happenings all over Jorius in the last hundred years and..."

"Let me guess, it's almost been a thousand years," I said. The expression on his face gave me chills all the way down my spine. I wondered if he and Ryze had discussed any of this, or if both of them thought they were the only ones who believed in the missing courts.

Clearly, communication between the two of them needed some work.

"That's another reason I've been helping all those omegas. I think the Court of Dreams and the Court of

Shadows are about to reawaken. I believe they're about to unleash hells and we need to be ready."

He barely finished speaking when light flashed outside the window. A moment later, a plume of smoke rose into the sky.

11

———

KHALA

"Shit," Cavan muttered under his breath. "You'll have to excuse me."

I barely heard him. All I knew was a mass of confusion on the other end of three bonds. Chaos.

"Ryze," I whispered.

Cavan took a couple of steps towards the door, but stopped and whirled back.

"Ryze what?" he demanded. "He's not supposed to be in Garial." He drew his head back and stared at me. "How do you know?"

I blinked a couple of times.

Fuck.

"I..."

Cavan closed his eyes for a moment. Opened them again and sighed. "Don't tell me. Mating bond? I should have guessed." He shook his head. "It changes nothing. Stay here. I'll deal with you later."

"No. If he's in trouble, I'm coming with you." I followed him to the door.

"The hells you are." He put out a large hand to stop me. "I told Ryze to leave Garial. If he didn't listen, and got himself into trouble it's his own fault. I will deal with him."

"Not without me," I said firmly. If I had to freeze him to the spot, I would. I'd deal with the consequences of that later. I wasn't backing down. We both knew it.

"Just as stubborn as your mother." He exhaled out his nose in frustration. "Don't make me regret this."

"I can't make any promises," I said.

"I thought as much. Just in case." He put a hand to my cheek long enough to make me shiver. "Stay within five metres of me until I say otherwise."

I felt his order settle on me like a cloak.

"You realise that's unfair, right?" If alphas were good at anything, it was bossing me around.

He grinned briefly. "I do realise that. What's the point of power if you can't throw it about once in a while?"

"I'm starting to think Ryze was right about you," I said. "You are an asshole." Which made Ryze one too, because that's exactly the kind of thing he'd do too.

"That might be the only thing he's right about." Cavan opened the door and stepped out into the corridor.

He didn't even have to look back to see if I was following. The compulsion to obey dragged me along. I slowed to test the strength of it, but I was forced to stagger forward to keep up.

"Does this thing go both ways?" I asked. "If I ran back down the corridor, or fell down the stairs, would you have to follow me?"

"Don't fall down the stairs," was his only answer. He gestured for the guards to follow and trotted down as if he didn't have longer legs than me.

If I was still human, I would have tripped. I couldn't have kept up his pace. I suspected that was purposeful. If I was struggling, I could stay behind. All I had to do was ask.

So I kept going.

"What's over where that smoke was?" I managed to catch up and walk beside him, extending my stride to match his.

"The Summer Court barracks," he said in a clipped tone. "If Ryzellius is up to something, and you knew about it..."

"If he's up to anything, I have no idea what," I said. All I knew was that he planned to stay in Garial until it was time for me to leave. Unless the Winter Court needed him sooner, in which case Tavian would stay and keep an eye on me.

"Believe it or not, the High Lord of the Winter Court doesn't tell me everything," I said. "You saw me tell him to leave. Then he left."

"Or didn't leave," Cavan said. He looked over at me like he didn't believe a word that came out of my mouth.

Then he exhaled heavily. "An alpha doesn't leave an omega behind when there's a mating bond in place. Not if he can help it. I didn't account for that possibility. I could have ordered you to tell me everything, but I prefer the omegas to trust me. In my experience, force doesn't make people friends. You would have resented me."

"Yes, I would have." I wasn't sure whether I trusted him or not, but I certainly wouldn't have if he made me tell him everything, then acted on what I said. Pissed off with him or not, I didn't want to betray Ryze.

That alpha-omega power thing really did suck.

He led us out the back of the palace, to a wide yard, where he made a portal. On the other side looked like pure chaos, but half of the guards headed straight through.

Cavan and I followed close on their heels, with the other half of the guards behind us.

We stepped out into the barracks. Fae were

running this way and that, none stopping to give us a second glance.

A muscular Fae stepped out of a larger building made of some kind of matte black stone. He gave Cavan a nod.

"Brace, what's going on?" Cavan asked.

"We're not sure, my lord," Brace admitted. His tone was short, words concise. "A flash of light almost blinded many of us. We don't know the source of it. A moment later, a storage building went up in flames."

"None of those buildings are made of wood," Cavan said.

"No, they're not," Brace agreed. "They're not made of anything flammable. There's very little flammable inside."

"Stone doesn't usually burst into flame."

"Not usually, High Lord."

"Where's Ryzellius?" Cavan snapped at me.

"Close," I said. I couldn't tell where exactly, just a vague direction. "Winter Court magic can't—"

"No, it can't. Lead me to him."

He didn't make it an alpha order, but he could have. Doing what he requested was easier to swallow. Besides, I wanted to know where Ryze was and what the fuck he was doing too.

I felt around again, then headed towards the source

of the smoke, which rose thick and steady toward the sky.

I half-heard the conversation between Cavan and Brace as we went.

"Did you say Ryzellius is in Garial?" Brace asked.

"Evidently," Cavan replied. "My omega will lead us to him. If he's behind this..."

I ignored them and wove through a group of Fae, who looked as though they were waiting for orders from someone.

"Follow behind us," Cavan snapped at them.

I stepped around the corner of the building and stopped so quickly Cavan almost walked into the back of me. He put a hand on my shoulder to steady himself, then dropped it back to his side.

"Fuck." I gaped.

The whole building—what was left of it—was still smoking. If it had burned, the fire was out. What remained looked like a pile of melted stone covered in ice.

Ryze stood beside it, weary and slightly dazed. He leaned forward, hands pressed to his thighs. Vayne was next to him, a hand on his shoulder. Wornar stood a little apart from both of them, appraising the buildings to either side of the ruin.

"I look forward to hearing an explanation for this," Cavan drawled.

Ryze glanced over. "Well if it isn't High Lord asshole himself." He gave me a glance and a faint smile, clearly trying to downplay the fact we knew each other.

"I was going to say exactly that." Cavan smirked. "What did you do to my building?"

Ryze straightened up. "I stopped it from getting so hot it set the rest of the place on fire. You're welcome."

That explained the ice.

"Why did it need your help?" Cavan asked. He stepped closer to the building, a deep frown etched on his forehead.

"I have no idea," Ryze said. "We saw a flash of light, then the whole thing was glowing. Bright red and scalding hot. If I didn't know better, I'd say it was struck by a bolt of lightning and turned into lava."

"No court has the power over lightning," Brace said. "Much less melting rock." His eyes widened and he took a step back. "If the gods—"

"I don't think it had anything to do with the gods," Cavan said quickly, darkly. "Just an accident of some kind."

He obviously didn't believe that. "We'll get to the bottom of it." He didn't bother to hide the fact he still suspected Ryze was behind this. But not just Ryze.

Brace nodded doubtfully, but moved to wave the Fae back to their duties.

"It looks like we need to talk," Cavan said to Ryze. "Not here."

Before Ryze could answer, Tavian came trotting up, his face pink with exertion. Sweat covered his brow. He must have run from somewhere.

"Looks like I'm just in time for the festivities." He pulled up to a stop and smiled. "Is everyone in one piece?"

"For now," Cavan said. "How long that lasts is up to the three of you."

Tavian was visibly resisting the urge to contradict him, but also decided to keep up the pretence we meant nothing to each other.

"Don't look at me," Vayne said. "I saw the light and followed Ryze here. Like he said, the building was glowing red. It was getting brighter and brighter. Looked like it was going to incinerate the shit out of everything. Ryze brought in a bunch of snow and ice. Building sizzled like a bitch, but it cooled down pretty fast."

"I can't believe I missed that," Tavian grumbled. "That sounds incredible."

"It was," Ryze said. "Cavan has plenty of enemies, I'm sure it will happen again soon."

Cavan rolled his eyes. "You're not above suspicion yet."

"You don't think they did it?" I asked him.

"Not for a moment," he admitted. "But we can't talk about what might have here."

"You think it was..." I closed my mouth and pressed my lips together.

"We can talk about it back at the palace." He gave me a light nod. He looked pained, but added, "You three better come with us."

"Us?" Tavian mouthed, his eyes on me.

I shrugged. Just when I thought the situation couldn't get any more complicated, it did. If Cavan was right about the other two courts, they may all have to learn to work together.

Ryze looked from me to Cavan and back again. He seemed tempted to punch Cavan in the face. The fact we were surrounded by Summer Court soldiers and a melted building served as a pretty good deterrent. For now.

"I'll make a portal," Cavan said.

Ryze gestured vaguely. "Be my guest."

Tavian stepped over closer to me and spoke softly. "Do you think we'll get to find out which one of them has the bigger cock?"

I snorted a laugh. "Stranger things have happened recently."

"My money's on Ryze," he said. "But only because I've seen it before."

"It's as good a reason as any to bet on him," I said.

"You're not honestly standing there talking about the High Lords' cock size, are you?" Vayne asked us. He spoke louder than could possibly have been necessary.

Ryze and Cavan both turned to look at us.

Tavian grinned unapologetically. "It's an omega thing, you wouldn't understand."

I could almost feel Ryze and Cavan's temptation to share a mutual rolling of their eyes. Their hatred for each other stopped them. Gods forbid they'd have anything in common. Only, I suspected they were more alike than they thought.

Wornar's face was pink with the effort to keep from laughing out loud.

Cavan shook his head and made a portal beside us. As before, half of the guards that accompanied us stepped in ahead, and half behind.

I walked between Tavian and Cavan, Ryze and Vayne on our heels. Wornar trailed a few steps behind.

"Don't forget it was you who invited us here," Ryze said. "In case you decide we turned up uninvited and think it would be a good idea to have us executed."

"I'm not sure it isn't a good idea to have you executed anyway," Cavan said. "If I didn't have more questions than answers right now, I might indulge myself."

"Always the charming host," Ryze told him. "We

might be lucky enough to get some more relatively good cake."

Wornar chuckled. "We can only hope."

I glanced up at Cavan. "I feel like I should apologise for them. Well, not Wornar. I only met him a couple of days ago."

"Believe me," Cavan drawled, "I'm very familiar with them and their interesting sense of humour. I don't think anything exists in the world they won't make fun of. It's amusing for the first century or two. Then you spend the third and fourth centuries wanting to put an arrow in their eyes."

"The feeling is entirely mutual," Ryze said. "I can't tell you the amount of times I've almost—"

I cut him off with a sharp look. I didn't think I could put up with the needling for another day, much less a century or two. Something strange happened, and we needed to figure out what the fuck was.

They'd have to bury their animosity, not their blades in each other.

12

KHALA

Cavan led us into a sitting room and nodded for the guards to stay outside. Either he wasn't worried about an attack from Ryze or one of the others, or he didn't want what was going to be said to be overheard.

I managed to plop down into one of the armchairs before anyone suggested I sit beside them. The situation was tense enough already.

"Let's start with what you're still doing in the city," Cavan said to Ryze.

Ryze sat back and crossed his legs at his knees. "I think you know."

Cavan sighed. "You're absolutely convinced I'm up to something. And you don't trust that Khala is safe here."

"I know she's not," Ryze said. "Why did you ask if you already knew the answer?"

"I was hoping for some honesty for once in your life," Cavan told him. "Without the jester act."

"Who says it's an act?" Ryze shrugged. "You know the truth. That's all there is to it. We went to the barracks to get some answers and found more questions. Including the fact you didn't look surprised at what happened. Have you been training omegas to melt stone?"

Cavan stared at him for a hard minute. Then he burst out laughing. "If that was even possible, why would I have them do it to my own building?"

"Because it wasn't aimed at the building," Tavian said softly.

All of us turned and looked at him.

He explained how Illaria met up with him in the street and delayed him.

I remembered her from outside the barracks at the Winter Court. She was making eyes at Zared at the time. Thinking about him gave me a pang of longing. I felt for him down the bond and found he was alert and confused but not alarmed. Alive, thank the gods.

"You think whatever that was, was aimed at Ryze?" Vayne asked.

"Or you or Wornar," Tavian said. "Or all three."

Ryze raised an eyebrow at Cavan. "That's not suspicious at all, is it? You could take all of us out with one hit."

"While I'm as disappointed as you are that it didn't happen," Cavan said, "I wasn't behind any of it. You can ask Khala. I was with her when that light flashed."

"Yes, he was," I said softly.

"That doesn't discount the possibility it didn't happen on his order," Ryze said. "With a convenient alibi all of us would believe."

"Why would I send anyone to distract Tavian?" Cavan asked.

"You like omegas," Ryze said dryly.

"If I wanted you dead, you'd be dead," Cavan told him. "Much more quietly. You've known me long enough to know I wouldn't have my city in an uproar to take care of a couple of problems."

"That may be true, but I'm not naïve enough to think you don't want me dead," Ryze said frankly. "However, you didn't bring us here to make death threats or go over bullshit we've gone over a million times before. You have a theory about what happened. Let's hear it." He made a, 'give it to me,' gesture with his fingers.

Cavan glanced at me.

His look didn't go unnoticed. Ryze and Vayne's

bodies both stiffened. Tavian made a sound in the back of his throat. If there was anything between Cavan and me, they might rip him apart yet.

I caught Ryze's eye and held it. "He thinks the Court of Shadows and the Court of Dreams are about to reawaken."

The silence that filled was heavier than a pile of blankets. I half expected it to be broken with laughter.

Instead, Ryze tilted his head back. "Fuck."

My gaze met Cavan's. Clearly, he'd expected a different reaction.

"You believe they exist too?" Cavan asked carefully.

Ryze lowered his chin. "I've long suspected they might. During some of my wanderings, I've kept an eye out for their whereabouts. If they exist, I haven't found them."

Wornar, who'd stood until now, flopped down onto a wide sofa. "The legends say they had different magic to the seasonal courts. The ability to see the ghosts of the past and the future. To control dreams and minds. To create enough rain to make floods. Theirs was like the power of the gods themselves. The seasonal courts were terrified of them. But they hated each other and wiped each other out." He shook his head.

"Not wiped out," Cavan said. "Just hidden...somewhere."

"Don't tell me," I said. "They could harness lightning and melt stone?"

That did sound like something gods would do.

"Why would they target Ryze?" Vayne asked.

"Because I'm exceptional?" Ryze smirked sarcastically. "Maybe it wasn't directed at me. Or at Cavan. It might have been intended as a general warning. Unless there was something in that building they didn't want anyone to get their hands on." He quirked an eyebrow at Cavan.

"It was nothing but a storage building," Cavan said. "It would have been full of potatoes, grain and bed sheets."

"Maybe they're offended by cum stains," Tavian offered, his expression deadpan.

"While I'm sure everyone has the same dislike of those, that seems an extreme reaction," Ryze said. "The real question here is what do we do about all of this? Potentially, this has nothing to do with the Winter Court. Merely some random enemy of Cavan's. It might be a good time for us to leave." He placed his hands to either side of him and started to push himself to his feet.

"You're welcome to leave, but I think you know this goes beyond me," Cavan said. "The whole of Jorius has been on edge for years now. Waiting for something.

Now *something* is here. I can't see another explanation for what happened today."

Ryze sat back down and put his hands in his lap. "Neither can I. Khala said you suspect the courts will awaken? What do you mean by that? Winter Court legend is similar to what Wornar said. The courts were powerful and annihilated each other. I thought if I ever found them, I'd stumble onto ruins. Fascinating, certainly, but nothing more than the remnants of long dead Fae. From what you're saying, I get the impression you think otherwise."

"Summer Court legend says they only went into hiding for a thousand years." Cavan pressed his fingertip to his lips. "The Court of Dreams that is. No one seems to know what happened to the Court of Shadows, apart from their disappearance happening shortly after. According to Harel, Autumn Court legend has them building ships and sailing to the gods know where."

"One legend says the High Lord of one court fell in love with the daughter of the High Lord of the other. They sought to bind the courts to one another. Yet another legend says the opposite. They fell in love but her father forbade them from being together and the courts went to war. The truth may lie somewhere in between blood and biding."

"Or with neither of those," Wornar said. "We're

talking about thousand-year-old legends. Myths. There may be no truth in them at all."

"If I hadn't seen a bright light melt stone with my bare eyes, I may be inclined to agree with you," Ryze said slowly. "It seems clear there are forces at play here. Forces that either are or are not trying to target me or the Summer Court."

"Forces that have allies," Tavian said. "Illaria said she was working with some others. She also said she came from the Autumn Court."

"Are you sure Harel isn't up to something?" Ryze asked. "He seems eager for an alliance with you."

"I'm certain he *is* up to something," Cavan said. "Which is why I let him stay here. I trust him as much as I trust any of you."

"But you don't think he's involved in what happened today," Ryze stated.

Cavan pressed his lips together. "He's a sneaky prick, but I don't think he has that kind of power any more than you do. He's curious about the legends of the courts, but he doesn't believe they exist. He thinks they were always a myth."

"Is there any chance he's right?" I asked. "I mean, I know what happened today, but maybe there's some other explanation."

"Bored gods?" Tavian suggested.

"I'd sooner believe the gods are a myth than the two

missing courts," Cavan said. "There may be another explanation, but in the last half-century, I haven't managed to find one."

Ryze stared at him. "You've been worried about this for that long?"

"Not just worrying about it, *preparing* for it," Cavan told him. "Gathering resources." He nodded towards me.

"Omegas," Ryze said flatly. "You expect us to believe you've been doing that, not because you want to go to war against us, but because you want to defend yourself and your court against the possibility the Court of Shadows and the Court of Dreams might reappear?"

"You can believe whatever you want to believe," Cavan said. "I've seen the signs and decided to be ready. If nothing else, those women deserved better than the humans would have given them."

Ryze shook his head in disbelief. "You didn't think to mention this to the rest of us?"

Cavan was still for a few moments. When he spoke, his voice was low and tight.

"I fucking *tried*. None of you would listen. Not. One. You decided long ago I was the enemy. For reasons you've probably forgotten yourself. I wasn't going to sit idly by and let your apathy destroy us all. If I had to stand between them and the rest of Jorius by myself, so be it. At least someone would be doing something, rather than all of us sitting back and waiting to die."

Ryze did sit back then, in his chair. "If all of this is true—"

"It's true," Cavan said.

"If all of this is true," Ryze started again, "I think we have some talking to do. I'm not saying I believe you, but we all saw what happened today. Maybe it was an attack, maybe it was a warning. Maybe it was a flex. I don't think it was an accident. Unless they were aiming at the palace and missed. If you're the only one, as you say, who's been preparing for this, they're going to want you out of the way first."

"That's a distinct possibility, yes," Cavan said. "Which is another reason Harel is here. If we need to evacuate Garial, I need somewhere for my people to go."

"The Spring Court—" Wornar started.

"Is too close," Cavan said. "If Ryzellius was receptive?" He raised an eyebrow at Ryze in question.

"We'll take them, if it comes to an evacuation," Ryze said without hesitation. "Of course we will."

"It's easy to pretend to be magnanimous when you spent the last fifty years ignoring the warnings I've been trying to give you," Cavan said darkly. "But I appreciate it. I never intended to make my court a target. My only intention was to be ready."

Without thinking, I moved to sit beside him and put a hand on his arm. "I believe you," I told him. "We can do this. If we work together."

Ryze's eyes seemed fixated on my hand, but he nodded. "I think we should start at the beginning."

13

KHALA

"Can you believe all of this?"

While the three High Lords—Harel joined the others an hour or two ago — and Wornar and Vayne talked, Tavian and I sat on the sofa and listened.

At some point, he put his arm around me. I nestled against him. Only Cavan gave us a look, which both of us ignored. I didn't know what was going on there and it didn't matter right now anyway. What did was the slight possibility they might actually agree on what to do about the potential threat.

Harel said he didn't believe a word of it, while at the same time looking cagey as fuck. After a while, I realised it was his default facial expression.

Ryze and Cavan both seemed to think the threat was real, but neither would agree to anything the other one said, even though they might have been about to suggest the same thing themselves.

Wornar seemed to find the whole thing amusing. At first, I thought he'd take Ryze's side, but then every so often he'd agree with Cavan.

"I'm starting to think that lightning strike, or whatever it was, was strategically designed to create exactly this chaos and animosity," I whispered.

"To be fair, the animosity's been there for a long time," Tavian said. "I get your point though. It was enough to make us wonder about whether or not something is coming. Not enough to prove it."

"What would it take to prove it? Thousands of heavily armed Fae attacking the city?" I shuddered at the thought.

"They'd still blame each other before they got around to responding." He made a face. "They've had a long time to piss each other off and finely hone their animosity towards each other. Even Ryze and Wornar, who get along better than the others, still have their moments. And then, sometimes when Wornar agrees with Ryze, Thiron overrules him. It's all a bunch of messy, political shit."

"We could be invaded and all they would do is sit around and argue?" That didn't sound like great leadership to me.

"Sooner or later, one of them would take a stand.

Then the rest would have to, because they wouldn't want him to take all the glory. Their egos wouldn't let them sit by and do nothing."

"And how many people would be dead by then?" I asked.

"A few hundred at least. This is why every now and again someone tries to overthrow one of them. Ryze is one of the better ones. Thiron too."

"Cavan doesn't seem as bad as you said," I said carefully.

Tavian's shoulder moved against mine when he shrugged. "I can't say I know him well. If what he said about his reasons for bringing the omegas here is truthful, maybe he's not. He's certainly good to look at." He glanced over at the golden haired High Lord and sighed.

I couldn't deny that.

Cavan and Ryze looked like night and day sitting at the same table. Ryze all in black with dark hair, Cavan in light coloured clothes and blonde. Both were undeniably attractive.

Vayne too, although he scowled at everyone. He looked about ready to tell them all to shut the fuck up and take over the meeting.

"What would Ryze think if he heard you say that?" I asked.

"Are you really asking what he'd think if he knew

you were thinking it?" Tavian's fingers grazed lightly over my hip. "I've noticed the way you and Cavan glance at each other. Ryze and I, we worry about you because neither of us want you to get hurt. I'm not saying we're not the possessive type, because we are, but if an omega wants someone in her pack, then who are we to deny her that?"

"Even though Ryze hates his guts?" I asked.

"Maybe it's past time they put their shit behind them. Failing that, at least things will be interesting." He laughed softly.

"And by interesting do you mean them trying to kill each other any chance they get?" I winced. The pair seemed determined to stab each other with words right now.

"That won't be boring, will it?" His smile widened.

"Is this one of those, 'when you've lived as long as we have you'll do anything for entertainment,' things?" I asked. "Because I might start to think all Fae are a little bit out of their minds."

"Only a little bit?" he teased. "Sweetheart, most of us were a little bit out of our minds two centuries ago. We're a long way past that now."

I exhaled softly. "I didn't want to be the one to say it, but now you mention it..."

He chuckled. "It's part of our charm."

"I suppose it gives me something to look forward

to," I said. "Being so bored I hope someone will stab someone else. I'm surprised you're not more excited at the prospect of an invasion. That would certainly break the monotony."

"That's going to the other extreme," he said. "Too much stimulation. The occasional fight is enough."

"You can't be serious?" Harel said loudly from his side of the conference table. His face was almost as red as his hair. "There's no such thing as either of those courts. Why do you insist on perpetuating this ridiculousness?"

I wasn't sure who his words were directed at, specifically. He seemed to be looking at Ryze and Cavan, and to some extent, Wornar. Vayne, he ignored altogether.

Vayne seemed more than happy with that arrangement. His scowl toward the High Lord of Autumn was deeper than it was for the rest.

"Go down to the barracks yourself," Cavan said evenly. "If you can tell me another way that building melted, I'd like to hear it."

"Along with a list of suggestions on how to prevent it from happening again," Ryze said. "Unless you deem it to be a random event, unlikely to ever occur again."

Harel looked less than pleased that both of them seemed to be ganging up on him.

"I didn't come here to be insulted." He glared at

Ryze, then at Cavan. Then at Wornar for good measure.

"Didn't you?" Ryze asked. "Personally, I've always found this a good place to come to be insulted."

"I thought you came here to dispense insults." Cavan regarded Ryze from half-lidded eyes.

"That too," Ryze agreed. "You make it so easy."

Cavan smirked. "If we can get back to the matter at hand."

Ryze sat back and spread his hands. "To summarise, Harel doesn't believe a word you said. I believe somewhere between a quarter and a third of it, because I saw the building melt. There's definitely some shit going on. I have no idea what Wornar believes."

"I believe I have to hear you out and then take all of this back to my High Lord," Wornar said. "Thiron will tell me what to believe."

"It might save time to have him come here," Vayne suggested.

"He'll want me to make sure he's not wasting his time," Wornar said, slightly apologetic. "You don't think anything will happen in the next day or two?"

"I have no idea." Cavan looked frustrated. He clearly knew this would be difficult, but the others weren't making it any easier.

Ryze looked almost as frustrated. He'd seen the

building melt, but to believe everything Cavan said after so many years of mistrust, miscommunication and the gods knew what else, evidently that was a stretch.

I knew he knew how to make a bridge and get over it. Apparently that was easier said than done.

"It could happen in the next minute," Cavan said. "No one foresaw what happened today."

"Except that woman from the Autumn Court." Ryze levelled an accusing look at Harel.

"Alleged woman," Harel snapped. "Did anyone else see her?"

Tavian's body stiffened slightly. I suspected no one noticed but me.

"Are you questioning the integrity of my Master of Assassins?" Ryze's tone was dangerous.

"I question the integrity of anyone who has ever shared your bed," Harel said scathingly.

"I was right," Ryze drawled. "You are here looking for omegas to fuck. Evidently the women of the Autumn Court have better taste than to share yours."

"He's not wrong," Tavian whispered in my ear. "Anyone can do better than him."

I bit my lip to keep from laughing, but I silently agreed with Tavian. Even in the middle of heat, I couldn't imagine choosing Harel.

Whether he heard us, or sensed we were talking about him, Harel turned and gave us both a dirty look.

"What are they doing here? Neither of them belong in this room."

"Tavian was a witness," Ryze said. "And I don't trust anyone outside this room with my omegas." His gaze settled on me and he offered me a faint smile.

"Khala was also a witness," Cavan said. He looked at Ryze like he wanted to start a whole new argument about whose omega I actually was.

"So they have answers as to what caused the so-called building melting? Otherwise I see no reason for their presence." Apparently my safety was of no concern to Harel.

Ironic, because I didn't give a fuck about his either.

"They might have insight you don't," Ryze said. "Especially in light of the fact you didn't see the building at all. Perhaps we should adjourn this conversation until he's done that. You never know, he might figure it all out for us." His tone was dripping with sarcasm.

Vayne snorted loudly.

Wornar grinned.

Cavan pressed his finger to his lip so hard the skin on both turned white. He was clearly struggling not to lose his shit.

I had to give him credit for not giving in and setting everyone else at the table on fire.

"I think it would be wise for you to look for yourself," Cavan told Harel. "I can take you there, if you prefer. I'm sure you wouldn't want to jeopardise the work we've put into building our alliance." There was definitely a thinly veiled threat in there.

Harel looked as though he was ready to stand up and stalk out. Instead, he sat back and crossed his arms over his chest.

"I will look at this building of yours. It may be I have the answers you seek. All of this conjecture about —" he waved his fingers dismissively, "—missing courts, may be all for nothing. I don't know about any of you, but I have better things to occupy my time with than myths and the kind of tales ignorant humans spread."

He looked around the table like they were doing nothing more than sharing a beer and bullshit stories.

"Yes, wouldn't want to waste your precious time, Harel," Ryze said. "Shall we go then?"

"There's no need for you to accompany us," Cavan told him. "I'm sure you also have better things to do."

"Not at all." Ryze smiled. "I'm sure Wornar would like to come too. Wouldn't you, Wornar?"

Ryze clearly had no intention of letting Harel or Cavan out of his sight.

"I should be there," Wornar agreed. "In case you find something I need to know about." Evidently he had the same intention as Ryze.

"All right then." Cavan rose. I couldn't tell if he was irritated or not. I presumed he was ready to do whatever it took to get the other High Lords to listen. He looked over at me and nodded.

"Khala, you can stay here." When he spoke, I felt the order to stay close to him lift from me. I hadn't realised how heavy it was until now.

"Khala would be safer with Tavian and Vayne," Ryze agreed.

"She can return to the atrium." Cavan's tone allowed no room for argument. "I don't trust that your men won't take her when we're not here." He'd already explained that he wanted me to stay because of my magic, and the need to learn how to use it.

I suspected there was more to it than that. A lot more.

Ryze clearly thought so too. "There's no need for that. She won't be staying when I return to the Winter Court."

Cavan cut him a look. "That's her choice."

Ryze returned the look. "Really? Because I got the distinct impression you thought otherwise."

"Can we get this over with?" Harel snapped. "Argue over your whore later."

Wornar actually took a step back when every single eye in the room turned to Harel.

I slapped a hand down onto Tavian's when he twitched like he was going to reach for one of his knives.

Cavan and Ryze both looked ready to punch Harel in the face.

Vayne's face turned pink. For once, he didn't seem to have any words.

Me, on the other hand...

I stood, keeping a hand out behind me for Tavian to stay seated.

I walked towards the High Lord of Autumn, looked him in the eye and said, "Fuck you." While he spluttered, I added, "For the record, I wouldn't. Not if you were the last man in Jorius. Or Fraxius, for that matter."

"As if I'd touch a woman with human blood tainting her," he sneered. "Filth."

His eyes widened as a knife flew so close to his head it must have shaved a couple of hairs before it embedded in the wall behind him.

14

KHALA

"*I* wasn't aiming to hit you," Tavian growled. "Next time I fucking will."

Harel quivered with rage. He barely turned his head to glare at Ryze. "Are you going to stand there and let your Master of Assassins threaten me?"

Ryze looked back at him, the soul of innocence. "I didn't see or hear anything."

"Me either," Vayne said.

"I'm staying out of it," Wornar said. "For the record, I'm almost certain I didn't see anything."

I turned to look at Cavan. If only because Ryze was playing innocent, I thought maybe he wouldn't.

He sighed and shrugged one shoulder. "That knife was already there, I'm sure."

I looked at Harel and smiled. Asshole.

He glared back. If we were alone, he'd slap me. I

saw all of that and more on his face. Disgust and hatred were present too, in equal measures.

"We've wasted enough time here. Show me your melted building." His gaze slid away from me.

I had the distinct impression Cavan wanted to tell him to get the fuck out of his court. If there wasn't so much at stake, maybe he would.

Instead, he nodded graciously and stepped over to an empty section of the room to make a portal. He turned to me, but Ryze got there first.

"Stay here in the palace until I return. All three of you." The order would only settle on Tavian and I, but that was enough. We both gave him a look but nodded as if we had a choice.

Tavian muttered something that sounded like, "Fucking alphas," but he slipped his hand into mine. "We'll take care of her for you." He even went as far as to smile at Cavan as well as Ryze.

If it was his job to stir up trouble, he was doing it well. If he wasn't careful, someone might use his knife on him.

"I'm sure Vayne will take care of both of you," Ryze said. "Won't you, Vayne?"

Vayne looked us up and down. "Pretty sure they can take care of themselves. And cause me less trouble than you do."

Cavan grinned.

Ryze rolled his eyes. "Do your people give you as much trouble as mine do?"

"No. Insolence like that is usually reserved for a special kind of pain in the ass," Cavan told him.

"Ohhh." Ryze drew the word out. "Yours give you *more* trouble than mine do, then."

"Hurry up," Harel snapped. He stepped through the portal first.

"Anyone else wish the other end of that was the bottom of the ocean?" Tavian said softly.

I raised my hand.

I'd been called all sorts of things throughout my life: trouble, stubborn, difficult. Never filth. Even Hycanthe hadn't gone far enough to call me a whore.

It wasn't just the names, it was the derision on his face. Like I belonged in some isolated cave somewhere no one could look at my face. He made me feel uncomfortable in my own skin. As if I wasn't struggling with who I'd become as it was.

Tavian grinned. "That's my girl."

Both remaining High Lords gave him a look before they followed Wornar and Harel through the portal to the barracks.

Cavan gave me a longer glance, and a smile before he closed the portal behind them.

"Don't worry about Harel." Tavian led me back over to the sofa and we sat back down. "He's the worst of them. He's bitter because no one likes him, but no one likes him because he's bitter. As far as I can tell, he's always been like that."

"He certainly seems aggravated and aggravating," I said. "And determined not to believe anything Cavan or Ryze said. I get the distinct impression it doesn't matter what they say or show him. It'll only be when strange Fae from previously missing courts turn up on his door that he's going to believe any of it."

Vayne sat in the chair opposite us. "The worst thing is, he'd probably join them to spite the rest of us. Same reason he's here to begin with. An alliance with the Summer Court just to piss off Ryze and Thiron. There's probably some other agenda in there too. That's a bonus of being an irritating piece of shit."

"He makes you look like you come from the Court of Rainbows," Tavian said.

"There's a Court of Rainbows?" I asked.

"No, but there should be. What in the world could be more amazing than rainbows? Imagine the magic. We could make rainbows appear everywhere. Or make everything more colourful."

Vayne made a gagging gesture with a finger in his mouth. "The next thing you'll say is that it'll make everyone so happy they'll dance in the streets or some shit."

Tavian snorted. "That would be going overboard. I want to make things prettier, not boring."

"That sounds better," Vayne said. "You could distract people with rainbows, then cut their throat."

"I'd be living the dream then," Tavian sighed.

I shook my head. "More than a little bit out of your mind."

He grinned. "If I'm out of my mind, then I don't want to be in my mind." He stopped and frowned. "I don't think that's quite what I intended to say."

"Sounds right to me," Vayne said. "I wouldn't want to be in your mind either."

"No, you'd prefer to be in my mouth, wouldn't you?" Tavian smiled at him.

"I'd prefer to be in her mouth." Vayne nodded at me.

"How much time do you think we have?" Tavian asked. He glanced at the space where the portal was only moments ago.

"Since when did you care?" Vayne asked.

Somewhat hypocritical, since he'd fucked my mouth in the training yard where anyone could have walked up and seen. In fact, Zared had seen out the window.

He told me that right before fucking me up against the door in another building. That seemed like a lifetime ago. The ache of not having Zared here with us burned through me like a physical pain. Like part of me got ripped away, in spite of the bond which still held between us.

I hadn't told anyone about that. I don't know why. Maybe because it was my little secret to keep. Some personal, private part of myself between me and him and no one else.

"Is it possible to reverse memory changes?" I asked. "I mean, if my memory was changed before I went to the temple, but I'm remembering things from before, does that mean they're not gone? They're just...pushed down somewhere."

They exchanged glances.

"It's not a Winter Court magic thing, so I don't know how it works," Tavian admitted. "Most people don't, given it's a rare ability. Someone like Dalyth would know better than we would."

I wrinkled my nose. The last person I wanted to ask about anything was her, especially because she'd know exactly why I was asking.

"I suppose I could ask her to teach me how to do it," I conceded. "Maybe she'll let something slip."

"Fuck," Vayne said. He sat forward, hands on his thighs. "You want to change Zared's memories back?"

"Of course I do," I replied. "Don't you think he deserves the right to choose where and how he lives his life?"

"Not necessarily." Vayne held up a hand before I could protest.

"I hate to agree with anything Cavan and Dalyth did, but he might actually be happier living his life the way he is now. He's going to grow old and die along with people who will do the same at the same pace. We all know what he'll choose if he's given a choice. He'll choose you. Maybe him too." He jerked his head towards Tavian. "You might take his whole life away from him. You might not give him the choice you think you are. You both might come to regret it. How will you feel when he hates you for giving him back something he might be better off without?"

I looked over to Tavian as he shrugged.

"I don't know if you're right, or if Vayne is. I'm a big believer in choice, but I also care about Zared, and I don't want to see him hurt. I don't want to see either of you hurt. As decisions go, it's one of the more impossible ones. One thing I do know, though, it's not one that needs to be made today. Think it over. Talk to Ryze. Talk to Cavan if you have to. I'm sure if you ask, they'll take you to Havenmoor or wherever Zared is so you can see how he's doing."

He took my hands in his. "I only ask one thing. Don't rush into this. All right?"

I nodded. "I won't." They were both right. I owed it to Zared to think this through and make the right decision for him. If that meant leaving him to live his life, then that's what I'd do. Even if it broke my heart to do it. Better my heart get broken then have his life shattered all over again. He'd end up hating me and that would devastate both of us.

When the time came, I'd have to think very, very carefully. And put my faith in the gods that I'd make the right choice.

15

KHALA

The four men returned after around an hour, with apparently nothing changed between them. Harel looked as pissed off and disbelieving as before. The other three didn't seem to have come to any sort of agreement.

They settled in for what looked like a full night of conversation, or rather arguing.

I excused myself and returned to the atrium.

The guards were back on the door, but I got the impression they were there to keep out anyone who shouldn't be there, rather than to keep us in. A move, presumably on Cavan's part to gain our trust. Or mine, anyway.

Maybe it was easier than having Tavian throw knives at them to get to me.

In the end, I went to bed with a restless mind and

more questions than I could imagine getting all the answers to. Including whether or not I was going to stay here, return to the Winter Court, or go somewhere else.

At some point, I needed to sit down with Ryze, but for now my priorities were up in the air. Getting my sisters out of here no longer seemed viable. If none of the other High Lords agreed with what Cavan was trying to do, and if those lost courts did in fact awaken, they'd be needed here. *I'd* be needed here.

I also wanted to be where my pack was. And where Zared was, all at the same time.

As far as I knew, I couldn't split myself in three.

I was still awake when the door opened slowly, almost silently. I assumed it was Tavian until I heard Ryze's voice.

"Khala? Are you still awake?" His whisper was soft enough that it wouldn't have woken me if I was asleep, but loud enough to hear.

"Yes." I sat up and rubbed my eyes. "Is everything all right?"

He took his hand away from in front of a lit candle, illuminating the room just enough for me to see him. He set the candle holder on the table to the side of the room and sat on the side of the bed.

"I feel I should apologise for... I'm not certain

where to start. I never intended for you to end up in the middle of all of this. In the middle of anything."

He rubbed a hand over his face. "I don't know what to think about what Cavan said. If he's right—if he's been right all along, we all should have been doing something for the last couple of decades. How many omegas with the magic we'll need didn't make it past their heat?"

"You believe what he says, don't you?" I asked softly. "You don't want to, because you don't like him, but he makes sense."

"He does, because I've always thought the two courts still existed somewhere." Ryze lay down beside me and placed his hands under his head. "Those maps, the songs, they have to mean something. I don't know... It's possible they annihilated each other and all of this is for nothing."

"I'm new to this magic thing, but I don't think nothing melts stone." I found myself snuggling into him. He draped an arm around me.

"The only thing I know that can melt anything that hard, apart from extreme heat, is you," he said. "I'm talking about hearts of stone like mine. Like Cavan's too, unless I'm completely misreading the signs. Which I might be. I seem to be excelling at misreading things lately. Like the last hundred years or so. There's nothing more stubborn than a Fae who gets stuck in a comfortable rut."

"I'm sure there isn't," I agreed. I wasn't sure about melting anyone's heart. Mine was confused enough.

"It's possible he's wrong about the courts, but he mentioned other things happening. Tavian said assassins went missing. And then there was Illaria. Why would she keep him from the barracks if nothing was going on? Everything would seem to suggest... I don't know what it's suggesting."

"Therein lies the conundrum," he said. "No one knows. We talked for a long time and came to no conclusion. Except that Harel is a bigger prick than I thought he was. I suspect we can all agree on that. That's another thing I'm sorry for. He shouldn't be calling you names. I wanted to rip his head off. I wouldn't have shed a tear if Tavian landed that knife in his brain. Although, if it would have further complicated an already complicated situation. You can't assassinate a High Lord without consequences. Whoever inherited from him would be obligated to return the favour and assassinate me. And then my cousin Johah would have to do the same thing. If you ever assassinate one of us, make sure the finger points at someone else."

"I'll bear that in mind," I said. "You didn't tell Cavan about the maps, did you?"

"No, I didn't," Ryze admitted. "Believing he might be onto something and trusting him are two different things. I can't rule out the possibility he's working with someone else. He might have found a way to combine several kinds of magic to create that lightning bolt or whatever the fuck it was. He could have tried to use it to get rid of me. No one would know which way to point the finger then."

He toyed with my hair lightly. Every so often, his finger would brush against my skin, making me quiver.

"He might have found one of those lost courts," Ryze said thoughtfully. "He said the Shadow Court hated the Court of Dreams. The Court of Shadows was the one, according to legend, with the kind of power that could melt stone. They might be hunting for information on the whereabouts of the Court of Dreams."

"Like the maps?" I whispered. "You think he might be trying to figure out who has those maps?"

"I can't discount the possibility," Ryze said. "Those maps might give him—*them*, exactly what they need. The animosity between Cavan and Harel might be a pretense. An act to get us to trust Cavan."

"I suppose it could be true," I said carefully. "Cavan seemed sincere." I didn't want to believe he was using me after all.

"I'm sure he did," Ryze said. "People will do anything when there's a lot at stake. Don't forget what he did to Zared. And those priests back at the caravan. I know he explained his reasons, but those may be nothing more than pretty excuses."

If I didn't know what to think before, I was even less sure now.

"I suppose so," I said reluctantly. "This is all just so..."

"Yes, it is. That's why I came to apologise. You shouldn't be in the middle of all of this. You're not a knife or an arrow. You deserve better than to be treated like one. By the way, telling Harel to fuck off like that was the best thing I've seen in a long time. I wanted to applaud. I've been telling him that for years, but never with quite as much conviction. And the look on his face." Ryze chuckled. "I won't forget that anytime soon."

I grinned. "It felt good." My smile faded. "Unless, as you said, all of that was an act and I played right into it. The situation made Cavan look like he was on our side. Especially after Tavian threw the knife."

"That was my second favourite part of the day. Much more fun than seeing that building glowing red, and thinking at any moment now it was going to explode and take me with it. I was seriously rethinking my life choices for a while there."

This was the first time Ryze mentioned being afraid of anything. I hadn't even considered what he might have been feeling, standing on the ground, trying to cool the stone and keeping it from killing anyone.

"You really think the heat would have spread?" I asked.

"Without a doubt," he said. "Another minute or two, and the ground would have been too hot to stand on. Anything made of wood would have gone up in flames. Anyone standing there would have been incinerated."

"Including you," I said softly.

"Including me," he agreed. "And Vayne. I thought Tavian was closer than he was, but I was worried for him too. Don't tell anyone, but I was worried for the Summer Court Fae too."

"If you're not careful, people might start to think you're not an asshole after all," I warned.

He turned his face to look at me. "Shit, really? We can't have that happening. People might start to like me, or something ridiculous."

I hadn't realised how much I missed his amused expression until it was right in front of me. He didn't take anything too seriously for long. On the surface anyway.

Inside, he took everything a lot more seriously. His humour was a way to conceal that. In the end, Ryze would do anything for his people, the same way Cavan would do anything for his.

Or would he? Shit, I didn't know what to think about Cavan right now.

"Trust is a precious commodity," Ryze said softly, as though reading my thoughts. He must have sensed them through the bond. Or he was that astute. Maybe both.

"Once it's lost, it's difficult to get it back again. But it's the one thing we should try never to lose, or take for granted. If I could go back again and do everything over—"

"I know why you did what you did," I said. "I was pissed off at you for not telling me everything, but I understand. And you're right, I would have freaked out. I would have been terrified of my heat. That might have all been for nothing. You did it to spare me. Honestly, if you had told me and I didn't transform, I would spend the rest of my life thinking what if it happened at the next heat, or the one after that."

"I've never heard of that happening, but I can understand why you'd think that way. No one ever said brains were logical. Sometimes they tell us things that aren't true."

"Like trusting Cavan?" I asked.

"Or mistrusting him," Ryze said. "I stand by every decision I've ever made as High Lord, but this one... This one might come back to bite me on the ass. No matter what I do, I might end up screwing us all."

"Is there any way to know what the right choice is without jumping straight in?" I asked.

"There might be," he mused. "Does this mean you're not angry with me anymore?"

"I'm not as angry as I was," I said. I couldn't go too easy on him. He wouldn't want me to anyway.

"It's a start." He lowered his mouth to mine and kissed me. Tentative at first, as if he thought I might slap him for it. Deeper when he went unslapped.

"What are you going to do to make it up to me?" I asked between kisses. Every time our lips met, my body burned a little more. It wasn't just the alpha-omega connection. It went far deeper than that.

I wanted him because I cared about him. Through the bond, I felt his emotions. In a matter of moments, I could barely tell my need from his.

"I can think of a couple of things. Do you trust me not to hurt you?" He pulled back and looked at me intently.

"Yes." I wasn't sure what I was getting myself into, but I knew he wouldn't. Not deliberately.

"Good." He grabbed the hem of my shirt and pulled it up over my head. He tossed it aside. "Roll over onto your stomach." He climbed off the bed and walked over to pick up the candle.

A spike of nervous excitement buzzed through me but I rolled over.

He sat back down beside me, legs tucked under him.

"One advantage to Winter Court magic is the ability to prevent people from burning badly."

In the centre of my back, a patch of cold grew. He held the candle over it and waited.

The wax dripped from the candle onto my skin. One careful drop at a time. Where it landed warmed my skin again, almost to the point of pain.

"Do you like that?" he whispered.

"Yes, I do," I whispered back. It felt fucking amazing. "You can make it hurt a little more if you want to."

"That's my omega," he said approvingly.

Once again, he made a patch of my skin cold, but not as cold as the first time. The hot wax made a pleasant sting against my bare skin. Each drop sent a surge of heat to my centre.

I hummed with pleasure. "Hotter than that. Please."

"Good girl," he said. "Needy and polite. I can give you everything you need. Even if you don't ask nicely." He chuckled.

He held the candle over my shoulders and let the wax drip without cooling my skin first. Each drip was an exquisite point of pain that lasted only a moment. I knew he must have been cooling the wax so it didn't burn me, but left it hot long enough to feel incredible.

I moaned. "I had no idea that could feel so good."

He moved down and grabbed the top of my pants with one hand. He pulled them down just enough to expose my ass.

"Let's see how you like it here."

The first couple of drops were almost enough to make me come on the spot. The wax wasn't the only thing dripping at this point. My pussy was too.

"Oh my gods," I breathed. I'd never felt a sensation like this before. Exquisite pain while at the same time, the absolute knowledge he wouldn't let me come to harm. My trust in him wasn't misplaced.

He let a few more drops land on my ass, then rose and put the candle back on the table.

Before he sat back down, he pulled my pants off the rest of the way. He dropped them aside, then parted my thighs with his hands. He kissed his way around my ass, and down the inside of one thigh and up the inside of the other. He teased around my rear hole with his tongue, before finding my clit and licking with firm strokes.

I shivered under his touch. Wanted more and more.

I felt his need match mine. Knew his cock was hard and aching. He'd make sure my needs were met before he even thought about his. Through the bond, I knew all of that and more.

"You taste delicious," he told me. He pulled his face

back, rolled me over and bent my knees to open me out to him. "All the better to feast."

He lowered his head back down to me and put all his attention onto my clit.

I bucked lightly, slowly against his mouth before I came, pleasure was washing over me in a warm wave that included his response to my orgasm. He was more turned on than before.

I floated back down to earth, but he didn't stop licking and teasing my clit, his hands on my thighs to keep my legs open.

His eyes on mine, he watched as my desire rose again. My second orgasm was deeper and more intense than the first.

I flopped down against the mattress.

He lifted his face long enough to say, "I'm not finished yet." He went back to licking and sucking, his teeth grazing my clit, tongue sliding inside my pussy.

I thought I was done until he worked me up to a third orgasm. This one made me arch my back and shout his name to the ceiling.

He still didn't stop.

"Ryze, I can't—" I pleaded.

"Yes you can," he insisted, his voice muffled. "One more, like a good girl."

I almost pushed him away, but I knew he'd persist until I came for him a fourth time.

His tongue must have been aching more than his cock, but he didn't stop, didn't slow. He worked me until my body felt like it didn't belong to me anymore. All I knew was his mouth on me and another rising flood of pleasure.

This time when I came, there wasn't a part of me that didn't feel it. Blood raced through me like a raging inferno, like dripping wax through my veins. Every bit of me was on fire, engulfed in pure sensation. The whole world could have ended right then.

Maybe it did. Maybe it shattered along with me in a burst of tiny lights, pants and moans.

Only when I flopped to the mattress, boneless, did Ryze move to kneel between my legs. I hadn't seen him shed his pants, or the rest of his clothes, but he was naked, lying over me. sliding his thick cock into my pussy.

This was the first time we'd been together outside my heat. This wasn't the frantic coming together that was; the primal urge to fuck.

This was slow, deliberate and careful. This was an alpha taking care of his omega, while satisfying his own needs. And me taking care of him.

I hooked my legs around him, rolled us over and straddled his hips. While I slowly moved up and down the length of his cock, he ran his hands from my stomach and up to massage my breasts.

"Has anyone told you you're perfect?" he asked.

"Not recently," I said. He was pretty fucking good himself. I rose all the way up to his tip, then lowered myself all the way down to his knot and his balls. His knot wouldn't lock outside my heat, it was still thick, and amazing.

"Khala, you're incredible," he said breathlessly. "Absolutely perfect."

"If you're not careful, saying things like that will go to my head," I teased.

"You're certainly going to mine." He closed his eyes and thrust up into me. "I don't mean the one on my shoulders."

I laughed softly. "I didn't think you meant that one." I started to ride faster, enjoying the way his breath became ragged pants. The way his fingers rolled and pinched my nipples.

"Such a good girl," he said. "My omega. My beautiful omega."

"My alpha," I said back. My feelings for Cavan were confused, but I knew what I felt for Ryze. He was my alpha. We were a pack. A pack who was missing one member, but I intended to fix that. One way or another.

He grunted, thrusting harder and harder, all the way inside me. He gritted his teeth and groaned.

"Gods, you feel incredible. So warm, wet and perfect."

He let out a low cry and came. Through the bond, I felt the way his balls tensed before exploding inside me in a rush of hot, pearly cum.

He flopped back down and tilted his head back, puffing lightly until he caught his breath.

"When is your birthday?" he said when he was able to speak again.

"My birthday?" I still straddled him, his cock still inside me. I could happily have stayed that way for hours.

"Yes, your birthday. I think I want to give you a crown." He looked up at me. "We don't have queens like humans do. We only have High Ladies if they rule. But I think you still deserve a crown."

"I don't need a crown," I told him.

"You might not need one, I still want you to have one. And if you won't wear it, I'll have to imagine." He half closed his eyes and smiled. "Even if it's only a crown of mist. Or smoke. Or starlight. Or a light dusting of snow."

"You're such a romantic," I told him.

He opened his eyes fully. "Not usually. You bring it out in me. Or maybe I am, but I've spent too long with Tavian and Vayne." He grimaced playfully, but it quickly turned back into a smile.

"You don't want to give Tavian a crown?" I asked.

"Now that's someone who'd actually wear one." Ryze grinned. "He'd want one made of knives he could pull out and throw. And stab people with."

"That would be practical," I said. "Something like that would suit him, except it wouldn't be very subtle." He'd looked fabulous in it, but it probably wasn't the perfect headwear for an assassin.

Ryze chuckled. "No, it wouldn't. I might hold off on ordering one of those to be made then." He gripped my hips and helped me off so I could lie beside him.

"Can I ask you something?" I snuggled close to him.

"Anything," he said.

"Are you sure? There might be things you don't want to answer." I pulled the blankets over us.

"If that happens, I'll let you know," he said. "Otherwise, ask away."

I straightened the blankets around our feet and lay back to get comfortable. I wondered if he was as surprised to end the day in my bed as I was to have him here. I had to admit, he looked good lying there, dark hair against the pale coloured pillows. Like midnight on snow.

"How does a pack add more members?" I asked. "You said it's unusual for one person to bond with four others. How unusual are packs?"

Apparently I had more questions than even I was

aware of. For every answer, I'd probably have a dozen more. Or a dozen-dozen.

Fae and human might not be that different, but throw in the whole omega thing and I had a lot more to learn. And a sneaking suspicion I'd still be learning in a decade or two.

"To answer your questions in reverse, packs are slightly less common than omegas. Some omegas prefer to be monogamous with one alpha. Some prefer one beta, except during heat. Some are lucky enough to surround themselves with several others who may be alphas, betas or omegas, like you."

"So having more than one alpha in a pack is normal?"

"It's normal in that it happens," Ryze said. "There's no right or wrong way to be a pack. They come together in whatever way works for the pack members."

"And if one member of the pack objects to another?"

"Then there's friction, but if they want to make it work, they will. Sometimes a pack member will tolerate another because they can't bear to be away from the others. Of course, it helps if everyone gets along. It's all a matter of communicating and being respectful. If either of my omegas wanted someone else that badly, it's my job to help them get what they want. For your sake or Tavian's, I'd tolerate almost anyone. Please don't tell me you've fallen for Harel?" He made a rude noise in the back of his throat.

I matched it with my snort. "Gods no. Almost anyone but."

I wouldn't go there with Hycanthe, Jezalyn or Geralda, the priestess from Ebonfalls, either. But I felt the way my body responded when Cavan touched me. I had a hard time putting it out of my head. In spite of everything, I found him intriguing.

Whether it would ever go beyond that, I didn't know. It certainly wouldn't if we found out he was playing us.

"What do we do now?" I asked. "Do we go back to the Winter Court and wait?"

"Actually, I have an idea," Ryze said.

I closed my eyes and listened to his deep, musical voice while he spoke.

16

―――――――

KHALA

I woke up warm, wedged between two bodies in my narrow nest. I inhaled the scent of leather and wood smoke on one side and cinnamon and apple on the other.

Ryze and Tavian.

I didn't know when Tavian slipped into the room. I had a vague memory of waking with his fingers on my clit, cock already inside me and a quick, almost frantic fuck before we both went back to sleep.

Movement caught my eye and I lifted my head as the door opened. Hycanthe peeked inside, gave me a disapproving glare and disappeared again.

Evidently, she hadn't gotten over her past prejudice against me liking sex. Or maybe it was the company I was curled up with. I dropped my head back down.

"Friend of yours?" Ryze asked sleepily.

"Sort of," I said. "I should talk to her." I reluctantly managed to untangle myself from them and quickly pulled on my clothes.

They both looked like they wanted to tug me back to bed, but they also got up and dressed.

We stepped out into the atrium just as the palace staff were serving breakfast. Neither man hesitated to grab some tea and toast, in spite of the looks the staff gave them.

The expression on Jezalyn's face was remarkably similar. The moment she caught sight of them, she put herself between them and Hycanthe. She and Ryze eyed each other, alpha to alpha. They reminded me of two angry cats, circling each other, sizing each other up for weaknesses.

Tavian looked appraisingly at Jezalyn, which earned him a scowl from Hycanthe.

Ryze seemed to find the whole thing hilarious. Of course he fucking would.

"Everyone relax," I said. "Jezalyn and Hycanthe are together. Ryze and Tavian are together. No one needs to be threatened by anyone else."

Jezalyn looked from Ryze to me and nodded. "As long as we understand each other." She took Hycanthe's hand and led her to sit down at the table.

I thought that was the end of it, but Hycanthe couldn't let it go.

"They don't belong here," she said. "Who are you?"

Someone like Harel would have been offended. Maybe Cavan too.

Ryze grinned.

It was Tavian who answered. "Allow me to present High Lord Ryzellius of the Winter Court. I'm Tavian, Master of Assassins."

"You shouldn't be here," Hycanthe told them. "Does Cavan know?"

I told her briefly about what happened yesterday and why the men were staying in the palace. Nothing I said wasn't information everyone here would know by now, so it wouldn't matter if the other omegas or the staff overheard. Evidently no one told Hycanthe or Jezalyn.

I didn't mention anything about the lost courts. I'd have to save that for when we were alone.

"I thought I saw a flash of light, but then I assumed I was seeing things," Hycanthe said. "Jezalyn didn't see it at all." There was something else she wasn't telling me. I saw it in her eyes. I couldn't tell if she also didn't want to share too much information in front of other people, or just me.

She surprised me by saying, "Can I speak to you for a moment? Alone."

I glanced at Ryze, who nodded.

"We'll be right out here enjoying breakfast." He bit into

his toast while watching Tavian, who'd sat himself beside another omega and was having a friendly conversation.

I followed Hycanthe to the room she shared with Jezalyn, and stood near the window while she closed the door.

"I wanted to talk to you, but you were...not alone," she said awkwardly.

I didn't want to get into that with her right now, so I jumped straight in. "What did you want to talk about?"

If she took me aside to judge me, I was going to be pissed off.

She glanced nervously towards the door, before stepping deeper into the room. It was the same size as mine, but reflected the fact they'd been here longer. The nest was full of pillows. Discarded clothing lay on the floor. It looked comfortably lived in.

"Something happened when the light flashed," she said. "Apart from some weird building melting. Just for a second or two, it felt like... Like a rush of magic through me."

She frowned, trying to put thoughts into words.

"I was stronger. It was as if the bit of me that's missing during classes was right there. I could have set the city on fire. And then it was gone."

She looked down at the white tiled floor. Kicked a sandal aside in frustration.

"Jezalyn believes me, but she didn't feel anything. Did you?"

I chewed my lip for a moment. Shook my head. "Nothing like that, no. Not that I recall. I saw a light, and then a bunch of smoke. Then I made Cavan take me down there with him. I didn't feel any burst of magic, just worry."

I told her about feeling Ryze and Vayne on the other end of the bond.

"I believe you," I added. I gave the closed door a quick glance too, before telling her everything else I knew. Everything except Ryze's plan.

"You don't think I had anything to do with that?" she demanded.

"No," I said firmly. "It sounds like whatever happened had some kind of impact on your magic. Have you tried using it since?"

"Yes, but it's as weak as ever." She sighed heavily. "It's as though none of that happened. I'm starting to think I imagined it."

"You didn't imagine it, but you should talk to someone who knows more about magic than I do."

"I'm not talking to Dalyth," she said quickly.

"I wasn't suggesting Dalyth," I said. "Ryze, or even Cavan. Either of them might have more answers than I do."

"Not Cavan either," she said. "I don't know if I can trust Ryzellius. He's one of them."

"A man?" I asked.

"A Fae High Lord," she replied. "I've seen Cavan and Harel. They all seem to have their own agenda and don't care who they use to get their way."

I couldn't argue the accuracy of her words. They did have their agenda, but who didn't right now?

"You can trust Ryze," I promised. "If you prefer, I can talk to him for you. I can try to keep your name out of it, but he knows we're in here talking."

She hesitated. "Make him promise not to tell anyone else," she said. Her mouth moved a couple of times before she continued. "Does this mean we're not leaving the Summer Court?"

"It might mean we're leaving sooner than I thought," I said. "But I'll let you know when I know." That was all I could give her right now.

She nodded and opened the door before following me out.

Ryze gave me a questioning look, but I shook my head. I'd tell him later.

"As much fun as this has been to spend so much time with so many beautiful women, Tavian, Khala and I are needed downstairs." Ryze gave the gathered omegas a bow and ushered us out the door.

Several of the women sighed as he left.

"You've still got it," Tavian told him.

"Do I?" Ryze asked. "I hadn't noticed." He slipped an arm around me. "I noticed you two."

We exchanged glances, rolled eyes and walked with him down the stairs and into another room where the staff were serving breakfast. As if they hadn't eaten already, both of them slipped into a chair and helped themselves to toast and eggs.

"How nice of you to join us," Cavan drawled from the head of the table. An empty plate set in front of him, but he was sipping from a delicate, porcelain cup. The smell of coffee mixed in with his eucalyptus and musk.

Wornar must have returned to the Spring Court. He was nowhere to be seen now.

"Isn't it though?" Ryze asked. "We thought about waiting until you left the room, but decided that would be impolite."

Both High Lords exchanged sarcastic smiles.

I slipped into a chair beside Ryze and reached for toast and black tea. I took my first bite when Harel finally shuffled into the room.

"Have any of you given up on the fantasy of the other courts?" He flopped heavily into a chair before reaching for three pieces of toast and a large pile of eggs. A member of staff poured him coffee, which he poked his finger into before half closing his eyes.

Judging by the steam that rose a moment later, he'd heated it.

"No we haven't, Harel," Ryze drawled. "Have you finally figured out what actually happened? I'm sure everyone around this table would love to hear it."

Harel shrugged. "I have no further explanation. Unless you believe in dragons."

"Dragons are a myth," Ryze said wearily.

"So are the Court of Dreams and the Court of Shadows," Harel retorted. "At least a dragon would explain the excess heat. Maybe it wasn't a light in the sky. Maybe it was a flash of fiery breath." He smirked. "It's as likely to be true as any other bullshit you've mentioned so far."

Tavian was staring at Harel. When I managed to catch his eye, he responded with a quick hand signal. "Later."

I couldn't tell if Ryze noticed, he seemed occupied looking lazily at Harel with a raised eyebrow. He stayed that way for a minute or two, then turned to Cavan.

"Quite some time ago in my library back in Lysarial," he said slowly, reluctantly, "I saw a map. It made mention of the Court of Shadows."

Cavan stopped with his cup halfway to his lips and jerked upright. "A map?" He echoed.

"For fuck's sake," Harel muttered. "More of this nonsense.

We all ignored him.

"I hadn't thought about it until now," Ryze lied. "It's vague at best. The general consensus was that it wasn't a map to a real place. In light of yesterday's happenings, perhaps I was mistaken in that assumption." Had he decided that they'd spend the rest of their days talking around in circles if he wasn't forthcoming about the maps?

"Perhaps you were," Cavan agreed. "This might be exactly what we need to find them. Can you bring the map here? Does it mention the Court of Dreams?" He was sitting forward eagerly, elbows on the smooth, mahogany table.

Ryze looked thoughtful. "There may be mention of the other court on another map. As I mentioned about the other one, it was vague. They may be no use at all, but I'd be more than happy to go and get them. On the condition Khala and any omega who wants to accompany her comes with me."

That spoke more volumes than the library contained about how he felt about me and helping my sisters. He was willing to share those maps in return for our safekeeping. I knew exactly how important those maps were to him. He'd kept their existence to himself for this long. I couldn't overstate how big a deal this was. To him, it would be like conceding a part of his court.

Cavan was visibly conflicted. He wanted to keep us here, but he needed to see that map.

"As long as they choose of their own free will," he said finally, as reluctantly as Ryze was to mention the maps. Another huge concession.

"If you're so concerned for their welfare, you're welcome to come with us," Ryze offered. "You're welcome to bring a few of your guards with you, in case you think this is an ambush."

Cavan clearly considered it might be. He thought quickly, then nodded. "I will accompany you. I'd like to see this map for myself."

"Excellent," Ryze said before turning to Harel. "Will you be joining us?"

"Hells no," Harel snapped. "It's long past time for me to return to my court. Send word when you're finished with this nonsense." He hastily finished his breakfast and stalked out of the room.

"If you'll excuse me, I have to take care of a couple of things before we leave." Cavan rose, nodded graciously and hurried out.

It wasn't until we were safely alone that Ryze turned to Tavian.

17

KHALA

"All right, what was that? The moment Harel mentioned dragons, you twitched." Ryze lifted his chin and regarded Tavian.

"I did not," Tavian protested.

"Something certainly happened," I said. "Are you about to tell me dragons are real after all?"

"Dragons—" Ryze started.

"Are a myth," we both finished for him.

"What was up with you?" I levelled my gaze at Tavian.

"I don't know," he said slowly. "When the light flashed, I had the impression of something. I thought it was ash, but then it was snow. When I put my hand out, I could feel it. But it wasn't in Garial anymore. I was on a field. Somewhere I didn't recognise. In the middle of a battle. Something flew over my head. I saw wings. White and grey with feathers."

"A griffin?" Ryze asked.

"That was what it looks like, but only saw a flash." His eyes glazed over as he thought back. "When Harel was talking about dragons, it came back to me. I realised something. Griffins can fly."

"That's not exactly news," Ryze said dryly.

"I know, but that light was in the sky. What if it wasn't a light? What if it was a portal? Opened by someone on the back of a griffin for just long enough to throw heat through before they closed it again?"

Ryze sat back. He pressed two fingers to his upper lip, and his thumb to his chin.

"Fuck. It may not have been aimed at me. It might have been an example of what they can do." He stood. "We need to get a look at that map."

"Yes we do," Cavan arrived back in time to see Ryze stand. Had he heard anything else? His expression gave away nothing.

"Perfect timing," Ryze said smoothly. "We were about to leave without you."

"I'm sure you were," Cavan told him, clearly not believing that for a moment.

Tavian pulled me to my feet and nudged me with his elbow. When I turned to him, he was grinning.

"What?" I asked.

"This is the bit where we get to watch two alphas argue over who's making the portal. It always gets interesting."

"I'm sure it does," I said. A smile tugged on the side of my lips. "Your portal or mine?"

He laughed. "That sounds perfectly inappropriate. Who wouldn't want watch them fuck each other?"

Before I could answer, I caught Ryze and Cavan staring at us both.

Tavian grinned broader. "It's an omega thing."

"If you keep saying that, I'm going to open a portal to that swamp we talked about," Ryze started. "Push you through it. And close it behind you."

"He wouldn't really do that," Tavian told me.

"I've heard he's done it before," Cavan said. He arched an eyebrow at Ryze. "Who was it? Someone spilled a drop of milk on your shoe?"

"If anyone spilled milk on my shoe, they'd deserve to end up in the swamp," Ryze said. "If you must know, they tried to kill me. Did you send them?"

"Not on that occasion, no," Cavan said.

"So you don't deny sending people to kill me?" Ryze pretended to be offended, but the humour in his eyes said he wasn't really.

"I'm sure you deserved it," was all Cavan said. "You

can make the portal. You know where we're going better than I do."

Ryze looked surprised but nodded. "Khala, are your friends coming?"

"They're already waiting outside," Cavan said. "Hycanthe, Jezalyn and a couple of others who are scared to stay in Garial after what happened yesterday. As soon as I stepped out of the room, I sent word to the atrium."

"How magnanimous and efficient of you," Ryze told him. "I'm almost impressed."

"I almost give a shit," Cavan said in return. "Actually, no, I don't. Not even a small one."

"Liar." Ryze nodded his thanks to Vayne, who stepped into the room carrying all of their packs. "You care about my opinion much more than you'll admit."

"Keep telling yourself that," Cavan said dryly. "That will never make it true."

Ryze smirked and slipped his pack onto his back before taking my hand. "Ready to go home?"

I wasn't sure how to answer that. I knew he wanted me to tell him I was, and that the Winter Court was home, but I wasn't sure I could say that yet.

"I'm ready to get back to my nest," I said finally. I knew he saw through my hesitation, and understood the reason for it. I also knew he'd do whatever it took to make Lysarial home for me. He squeezed my hand as we walked through the door together out into the open hallway.

As Cavan said, Hycanthe and Jezalyn were waiting there with two other omegas, a few guards and, to my annoyance, Dalyth.

"These three haven't finished their training," Cavan said. "I'm sure you'll agree it's important they keep up with that." He didn't look like he cared too much whether Ryze agreed or not. Like me leaving wasn't negotiable, neither was this.

"On the condition she returns here the moment they're ready," Ryze said. He turned away before anyone could argue, and opened a portal.

The same as the first one I ever saw him make, this one wound around a bend, the end disappearing out of sight. Garial and Lysarial were obviously a great distance apart.

Ryze pushed me gently towards Tavian and Vayne. "Stay near them. You three go through first. Cavan and I will go through last, so we can keep an eye on each other."

Cavan nodded, apparently satisfied with that arrangement. What would it take for those two to trust each other? Would they ever? They might need to, sooner or later.

Evidently, today was not that day.

To my surprise, Vayne took my other hand. The three of us stepped through together.

In spite of having done this before, I still expected it to be cold inside the portal. Like always, it was warm all the way through until we stepped out the other side. Not into the sitting room at the palace in Lysarial, as I expected, but rather in a yard near the kitchen.

We hurried to move out of the way of everyone else coming through.

I glanced around, half expecting to see Zared come running out to greet us. Possibly to stab Dalyth and Cavan for sending him away. Of course, he wasn't here. He was a long way from Lysarial. Closer now, according to the bond, but still too far from me.

"It's nice to be back here," Tavian said. He and Vayne seemed to be scanning the area, looking for trouble or anything out of place.

As far as I could tell, none of the buildings were melted, exploded, imploded, or otherwise impacted in any way. Everything looked just how we left it.

By twos and threes, everyone stepped through the portal. Ryze and Cavan still looked at each other dubiously until Ryze closed the portal.

"Would you like to get settled first, or shall we get straight to the library?" Ryze was asking Cavan.

"I see no reason to wait," Cavan said.

Ryze nodded. "I didn't think you would." He waved one of his staff over and told them to take care of Jezalyn and the omegas. And to find separate accommodation for Dalyth. Clearly he had no intention of taking her into the library.

She scowled, but went quietly when Cavan gave her a nod.

Another member of staff took everyone's packs. The rest of us headed to the library.

"This is impressive," Cavan admitted once we stepped inside. He tilted his chin and looked around, taking everything in.

"Everything is bigger and more impressive in the Winter Court," Ryze remarked.

Cavan snorted softly and continued his appreciation of the shelves and shelves of books.

Ryze shrugged to us and placed his hands on his hips. "Now, the maps are in this section."

Cavan had pulled a book off the shelf and was looking at it with raised eyebrows. "I didn't realise Winter Court Fae were as adventurous as those of us from the Summer Court."

"We're not," Ryze said absently, as he scanned the racks. "We're much more adventurous. Aren't we, Tave?"

"I don't know," Tavian admitted. "I don't have any experience with anyone from the Summer Court." To

Cavan he said, "Are you offering?"

Cavan's eyes slid to me. He gave me a smile which clearly said he'd extend me the offer any time.

My pulse actually fluttered.

I managed to look away, but not before I saw what page Cavan was looking at. I'd like to try that, whether it was him or someone else.

"Anyway, the maps." Ryze drawled. "If you don't mind." He stepped in front of us. "They're precious and brittle. You're welcome to watch over my shoulder."

That was exactly what Cavan did. I stood on the other side, Tavian and Vayne behind me.

Ryze carefully turned page after page, saying what each one was as he went. "Map of Lysarial. Map of the land surrounding Lysarial. Map of the Winter Court. Map of our border with the Autumn Court. Map of our border with the Spring Court. Map of..."

He tilted his head, and lowered his face for a better look. "Something so faded I can't make it out." He handed it over his shoulder to Cavan.

"That might be the swamp you were talking about." Cavan shrugged and handed it back.

Ryze looked again. "Ahhh, you might be right." He placed it with the others.

He kept turning over pages. They crackled under his touch and some of the corners started to split. He winced a couple of times.

After about ten maps, Cavan put a hand on his arm. "Wait. There. Right where you put it whenever you put it there. One day you might appreciate the fact I wasn't born yesterday either."

"I don't trust you," Ryze said simply. "Of course I'm not going to tell you everything straight away."

"One of these days, people will die because of that," Cavan says scathingly. He shook his head and turned his attention to the map.

"You were right about one thing, it is vague." He ran his finger down the centre of the piece of parchment. "Those mountains look familiar."

"They do?" For once, Ryze was sincere. "They don't appear on any map I've ever found. I've spent decades comparing them."

Cavan responded with a grunt of annoyance. "If you listened to me sooner, we might have found what we were looking for by now." He turned back to the map, tapped on it absently with a fingertip. "If I could just remember where I've seen a mountain formation like that."

"Somewhere there's griffins?" Tavian asked casually.

Cavan's finger stopped tapping. "What did you say?"

Tavian glanced at Ryze, who shrugged.

"I said somewhere there might be griffins," Tavian

repeated.

Cavan mouthed the words. *Somewhere there might be griffins.*

"What is it?" I asked.

"I think I know where this is," Cavan said.

18

TAVIAN

"**A**re you going to force us to guess?" Ryze asked. "Like I said, I've spent decades looking for where this is. I'm somewhat out of guesses."

He looked pissed Cavan might have the answers to questions he'd had for such a long time. We'd spent a good many nights drinking, talking and speculating about this.

Like with most things, Vayne thought it was a waste of time. I wasn't sure I disagreed with him, but it was important to Ryze. That meant it was important to me.

On those occasions he got it into his head to go searching for lost courts, I went with him. All we ever found were local legends from all over Jorius. When we weren't ducking Autumn Court border patrols and the like.

No one ever said life with Ryze wasn't fun.

"I'm only guessing myself," Cavan told him. "Obviously it's not in Jorius."

"I concluded as much," Ryze said. "I've never seen a formation of mountains like that in Fraxius either. I haven't spent much time in the lands beyond that."

"There are lands beyond that?" Khala tilted her head and looked up at him.

Like it did every time I looked at her, my heart skipped a beat. I'd never seen a woman as fucking gorgeous as her in my life. She smelled of lavender, fresh rain and omega sweetness. Between her and Ryze, my cock ached more often than not.

I loved every minute of it.

"Gerian and Freid," I told her. "Human land. Very unwelcoming to Fae. Even less than the Autumn Court is welcome to outsiders."

She turned her pretty eyes towards me. "Sounds like a good place to hide if you don't want to be found by other Fae."

"Not so much if you are Fae and object to being shot on sight," Ryze said. He looked toward Cavan. "That wasn't what you meant."

Cavan shook his head slowly. "Natanya."

Ryze, Vayne and I all stiffened.

Khala looked from one to the other clearly confused. "What is Natanya?"

"Some call it the forbidden lands," Ryze said. He

spoke softly as though not wanting to be overheard by the gods. "The land beyond the mists."

"Superstitious?" Cavan asked mockingly.

"When it comes to that place, yes, I fucking am." Ryze glanced back at the map. "I tried to go there once, when I was young and stupid." He shuddered.

"What makes you think the map is leading there?" Khala asked Cavan. "Apart from the fact hiding somewhere even Ryze is scared to go is potentially a good place to hide."

"I didn't say I was scared to go there," Ryze snapped. "I just said I've been and it freaked me the fuck out."

"There are records in the Temple in Havenmoor," Cavan said. "Specifically, a map carved into the wall. It dates back to when Fae occupied Fraxius. Before the seasonal courts were formed. Before the mists. On that map is a mountain range that looks like this." He tapped the map again.

"That could be nothing more than a coincidence," Ryze said.

"Or it might not be." Cavan straightened and crossed his arms.

"Are you suggesting the Court of Shadows put mist around itself to keep everyone out?" Khala asked. "That it was there all along?"

"Doubtful," Cavan said. "The mists appeared at

least a hundred years after the courts disappeared. But
the clues to their whereabouts might be there."

"Or they might be here." Khala leaned over the map
and read out loud.

"Court of Shadows, whispers creep,
Fae of darkness love to sleep.
Their magic like knives, eyes a-shine,
They lurk and hide, await a sign.

THE TREES here bend and twist and creak,
If they're alive, somehow speak.
Branches reach out with spidery claws,
Open the air, the harsh, cold doors.

FAE OF SHADOWS GATHER HERE,
Court of secrets, place of fear,
Dance and sway with subtle grace,
Shadows flicker on every space.

THE MOON IS ALWAYS FULL,
It casts a glow on the skulls,
That line the path and watch,
With hollow eyes, wary touch.

. . .

IF YOU DARE ENTER the court,

To find the ones long sought.

Fae here play a deadly game,

They'll ensnare you, hard as stone.

HEED THE WARNING CLEAR,

Those who wander too near,

The shadows, where the Fae,

Play games of darkness, night and day."

"SO POETIC," I said.

RYZE LEANED OVER THE MAP, beside Khala.

"If I didn't know better, I'd think they were suggesting we ask a tree for the answers. I've gone over that bit in my head a thousand times."

"To seek the Court of Shadows," Cavan read. "As if they're alive, they somehow speak."

"Trees don't talk," Vayne said. "How are they going to have any answers?"

"There's more than one way to speak," Khala pointed out.

"Yes there is," Ryze agreed.

"What does the other map say?" Cavan asked.

Ryze pulled out the other map. He unrolled it and placed it beside the first.

Cavan shook his head slightly and read:

"IN THE COURT OF DREAMS, Fae dance,
Hearts flutter in a wild prance.
The moonlight shines so bright,
Lighting steps that flow all night.

THE AIR IS alive with Fae song,
A place where dreams hold long.
The scent of honey and blooming flowers,
Mingle with the Fae's lost powers.

THEIR VOICES BLEND, sweet and true,
A melody that echoes through the hue.
They sing of love and endless wonder,
Hearts aglow, spirits thunder.

THE COURT OF DREAMS is a place of wonder,
Where Fae reign with magic stronger.
Come dance beneath the moon,
Lose yourself to the compelling tune.

. . .

IN THE COURT OF DREAMS, time stands still,

All around is magic and thrill.

Close your eyes and take a chance,

Join the Fae's wildest dance."

"That sounds like my kind of place," I said. "Music and dancing. Much more fun than trees trying to claw your eyes out."

"It shows the same place as the other map," Khala said. "If the two courts hated each other, then they weren't going to live on top of each other, right?"

"Right," Cavan agreed. He seemed to be lost in thought.

I couldn't deny how attractive he was. If Khala and I were able to coordinate our heats, we might have a lot of fun with both alphas. And Vayne. And Zared too.

Thinking about him made me as conflicted as Khala must have been. I missed him like an ache in my heart, but if he was content living his human life, then what right did I have to yearn for him at all? I should be happy for him. I wasn't, and that made me feel like a selfish prick, but it was what it was. No one ever said love was logical or even selfless.

We chose who we wanted to walk with on this road, and I chose him along with Ryze and Khala. Even if it wasn't meant to be.

"This might be nothing more to a clue as to the last spot they were before they wiped each other out," Vayne said.

"Or a warning to stay away," Khala added.

"Or a map leading to a huge vault where the treasure of those courts is buried," I said.

"I hate to say it," Ryze said, "but that seems unlikely. Although, it would explain why I have both the maps here. What other court could be trusted with a secret like that?"

"The other courts might be smart enough to solve the riddle." Cavan smirked.

Ryze raised an eyebrow at him. "Interesting theory, but with absolutely nothing to back it up." He smirked in return.

"We can all agree the Winter Court is a better place for them than the Autumn Court," I said.

"Under its current High Lord, yes," Cavan said. "Harel would have these burnt."

"If it means going into the mist, I'm not sure he'd be wrong to do that," Ryze said. "I like an intrepid adventure as much as the next man, or woman, but that place isn't right."

"You don't have to go if you don't want to," Cavan told him. "I'll go with a contingent of my people. If you're lucky, I might tell you what we find."

Of course that was exactly the thing to make Ryze respond to the way he wanted him to.

"I'm going," Ryze said firmly. He never could back down from a challenge or a dare. "But there's somewhere we need to go first. I'd like to see that map in Havenmoor. If we can match that with this, we might have a better idea where we're going."

"I'd like another look myself," Cavan agreed. "And for the songs on the maps to be transcribed. Unless you prefer we carry these around with us?" He waved his hand over the maps.

"I'll do it," I said. "I presume we don't want anyone outside this room to know about it?"

"I think that would be wise." Ryze nodded. "These maps are too fragile to remove from here. Make a sketch of the maps too, so we can take them with us to Havenmoor."

I nodded. "Khala, want to help me?"

"Of course," she replied. "On the condition I get to go to Havenmoor too."

No one needed to ask why.

The High Lords exchanged a glance. Ryze looked as though he was waiting for Cavan to say no. Cavan simply pressed his lips together, leaving Ryze to answer.

He looked at the way Khala's chin jutted out in determination and reluctantly nodded.

"Fine, but if we bump into Zared—"

"I just want to see if he's all right," she said quickly, firmly. "I want to see that map for myself anyway."

Ryze held up his hands in surrender. "All right. Get to work. We'll leave first thing in the morning."

I nodded and went in search of paper and something to write with.

By the time I returned, everyone left except Khala. She stood pouring over both maps, a frown on her pretty forehead.

I wanted to tear off her pants and fuck her over the table, just like that. But I had a job to do first.

"Do you think it is a riddle?" I placed the paper down beside the first map and started a careful sketch.

"It could be a silly children's song for all I know," she said. "The Court of Shadows sounds like a nightmare. The Court of Dreams sounds like, well, a dream. Do you think they really existed?"

I paused in my sketching for a moment. "Until yesterday, I would have said I don't know. Going with Ryze... It was something to do. You know? Indulging his fantasy of the glory of finding missing Fae or some shit like that." I shrugged one shoulder.

"And then yesterday?" she prompted.

"Then I saw griffins right above my head that weren't there. I have a good imagination, but this was something completely different. It was happening in front of me."

I'd smelled smoke in the air. Felt the rush of wings above me. I heard the screams of people dying, and the clash of steel on steel. I was right there. In the middle of a field of battle. Hells, I could even smell blood and fear. It coated the insides of my nostrils, heavy and thick. Several metres away, a man sobbed in agony before he twitched and felt completely still. His eyes stared up at the sky, accusing and scared.

The moment passed, I found myself standing in the streets of Garial, surrounded by people going about their lives. Nothing about it seemed real. It took me a solid couple of minutes to reorient myself again. To convince myself I wasn't really on a battlefield. I was nowhere more extraordinary than a street in the Summer Court.

"It's too strange to disregard anything at this point," I concluded.

"Can you keep a secret?" she asked.

"Sweetheart, I wouldn't be a good Master of Assassins if I couldn't," I told her.

She smiled and lightly kissed my mouth. Then told me about Hycanthe and her magic.

"Whatever happened yesterday, something happened to both of you." She looked worried, for her sister and for me. Not for herself. That was typical

Khala. She was beyond sweet. Especially when she told High Lords to fuck off. That was literally the best thing I've seen in years. That and the look on Harel's face.

I nodded, and said, "I think we should keep both of these things to ourselves. For now at least. We can trust Ryze and Vayne, but Cavan would feel obligated to tell Dalyth and fuck knows what that bitch would do."

"I trust her as far as I could throw a mountain with one hand," Khala said eloquently.

"What about Cavan?" I went back to sketching. "You wouldn't kick him out of your nest, would you?"

She smiled and laughed softly. "No, but that doesn't necessarily mean I trust him either. Physical attraction doesn't always make sense."

"Is that all it is?" I carefully drew the outline of the mountains, and shaded where the map was shaded. "He's also intelligent, powerful, and doesn't take crap from anyone. Not even Ryze."

"It sounds like you have a crush on him," she teased.

I looked over and flashed her a smile. "Is it that obvious?" I pushed my hair back over my shoulder and went back to sketching. "Like you said, physical attraction doesn't always make—"

Khala was gone.

The whole library was gone.

19

TAVIAN

The mountainside overlooked a wide valley. A sheer drop ended in a river, which meandered through the middle, glittering in the afternoon sun.

I traced its progress with my gaze until it reached the delta and flowed out to sea.

A stiff breeze ruffled my clothes and hair. Strands blew across my eyes. I pushed them back, tucking them behind my ears. I straightened my long tunic.

"Are you listening, Patric?" a voice snapped behind me.

I turned.

The man beside me turned too. "I hear you Yala, but it's not time yet. The chicks are too young."

"Old enough to be ridden," Yala snapped. "What are we waiting for? The next clutch of chicks? The clutch after that? You always say it's not time yet." Her eyes flicked to me and she curled her lip before looking away.

"When the time is ready, we'll know," Patric said patiently.

"Tavian?"

Whose voice was that? There was no one here but me, Patric and Yala.

"Tavian?" It came again, more frantic this time.

"How will we know?" Yala demanded.

"The five will come—"

Patric's voice faded and he was gone, replaced by the library and Khala's worried face.

"Tave? Are you all right?"

I shook my head. "Yes. I'm fine. I was just...not here for a moment."

"I saw that," she said. "You looked deep in thought, but your face was pale." She brushed hair off my forehead with warm fingers. "You're so cold."

"It was—"

The sound of screaming outside the library interrupted me.

"Stay here." When she started to argue, I grabbed her wrists and pulled her closer to me.

"Whatever's going on, someone needs to finish transcribing those songs and sketching the maps. Can you do that?" I looked firmly into her eyes. I needed her to do this. Ryze needed her to.

She nodded. "I can do it, if you promise me you'll be safe."

I kissed her mouth quickly. "I always do." I let her wrists go and started out of the library at a trot. I was used to dealing with all sorts of shit, but this had me on edge. Whatever I saw, whoever those people were, had something to do with this. I was certain of it.

I slowed to a walk before I stepped out into the sunshine.

Into chaos.

Like in the Summer Court barracks, Fae ran back and forth. There, it was from fear. Here, it was with purpose.

They ran to refill buckets, to throw water on fires that blazed in the trees and various buildings. Debris lay everywhere. Branches, brooms, random pieces of cloth, what looked like a smashed wagon.

I grabbed the arm of a young man as he ran past.

"What the hells is going on?" I asked.

"A huge whirlwind," he panted. "Came through from the sea. Grabbed up everything in its path and threw it around like it was nothing. Then it was gone."

"Any flashes of light?"

He gave me a funny look. "Not that I saw. I saw the wind and ran like hells until it was gone. Now it's got things on fire." He nodded towards another wagon, this one fully ablaze.

I nodded. "Go." I dropped my hand and he went on running.

I supposed it could have been a coincidence, an act of nature or the gods. My instincts told me otherwise.

I was about to head inside when a portal opened beside me. Ryze, Cavan and Vayne stepped out so fast Ryze almost barrelled into me.

He grabbed me at the last moment. "What the fuck happened?"

I told him what the young man told me.

"No winter magic can do that," he said.

"Not summer either," Cavan said. "A combination of it can."

"Khala was with me. She didn't do it," I said quickly.

Ryze eyed Cavan. "Where was Dalyth?"

"Training the other omegas," Cavan said coolly. "Hycanthe isn't strong enough to do something like this."

I wanted to contradict him, but not in front of Ryze and not after telling Khala I wouldn't say anything to anyone about Hycanthe's magic getting stronger during yesterday's attack.

"We don't get whirlwinds at random here in Lysari-al," Ryze said.

"I think we can all agree it wasn't anything random," Cavan said wearily.

"Nothing happened here yesterday," Vayne said. "I've spoken to my second-in-command, she said it was as boring as shit. If this was the same asshole as in Garial, then I suggest they're following one of you around."

"They might be following *you* around," I pointed out. "You are pretty cute." I couldn't resist the flirt, if only to see the expression on his face. He was too easy to rile.

Vayne snorted. "Yes I am, but they can fuck off. I'm not interested."

Ryze patted him on the shoulder. "You'd have to be slightly flattered if they've gone to all this trouble to get your attention. Wouldn't you?"

Vayne jerked away. "It's not about me," he growled. "Tavian was the one Illaria tried to keep away from the barracks. Maybe it's about him. Or you," he said to Ryze. He glared at Cavan but didn't say anything further. He didn't need to. It was obvious to everyone where he thought the blame really lay.

"Extreme heat and high wind," Cavan said thoughtfully. "Both destructive forces."

"So?" Ryze asked. "They haven't done much damage so far."

"Exactly," Cavan agreed. "It's like a hen pecking at a hunk of bread."

"A hen can't swallow a loaf of bread whole," I said. "All she can do is peck at it."

"Until what?" Cavan asked.

I frowned. "Until she manages to tear it apart. You think that's what's happening here? That if they nibble at us here and there, we'll tear ourselves apart?"

"Considering our struggle to remain civil to one another, I'd say they're assuming that will be the result," Cavan said. "Whether or not it is, is up to us."

"I think he's trying to tell you to play nice," Vayne said to Ryze.

"I always play nice," Ryze said. "But why do something different here than in Garial?"

He thought for a moment before he answered his own question. "They misjudged. They didn't think there'd be anyone in Lysarial who could deal with extreme heat. And they didn't think there'd be anyone here who could stop that wind."

"Khala didn't stop it," I said. "Either someone else did, or it stopped by itself."

"Dalyth might have," Cavan said. "But no one would have anticipated her being here in Lysarial. Whatever they're basing their information on, it's out of date."

"Or a bunch of coincidences," Vayne said.

"Or that," Ryze agreed. "If we can ascertain what

they think they know, maybe we can get ahead of them."

"If they think we're looking for them, chances are they'll know we'll go to Havenmoor," Cavan said slowly. "If they can only act once a day, we should go there now."

"They might be anticipating that we assume they can only act once a day," Ryze said.

"Whatever we decide we can assume, they assume," I pointed out. "Maybe we should be as prepared as we can."

"That goes without saying," Vayne said with a grunt.

"Why did you ask about the griffins?" Cavan asked me suddenly.

I glanced at Ryze.

He closed his eyes for a moment, then reluctantly nodded. "If they want us to tear ourselves apart, the best we can do is to not let them. Let's go back into the library."

Cavan regarded Ryze for a moment, but followed us back inside.

"Just in time," Khala said as we approached. "I've finished writing out the songs." She handed the paper with her neat handwriting on it to Ryze.

"I can't remember the last time I saw handwriting I could read so easily," Ryze said. He folded the paper and placed it into his pocket. "I'm so used to writing that looks like a spider was crawling along the page and got squashed."

"In other words, your own writing?" Cavan asked.

Ryze smirked. "No, not mine." He turned to me. "You might as well tell Cavan everything you told us. If nothing else, it will save him from complaining later about things he didn't know."

He leaned against one of the shelves, cocked his head and waved a hand to give me the floor. A faint smile graced his full lips.

Cavan smirked back. "You'll thank me when your court isn't in ashes." He turned from Ryze and raised an eyebrow at me. He was too attractive for his own good. Probably mine and Khala's too.

In as few words as possible, I told them what I saw both times. Standing on the battlefield and standing on the mountainside. They all listened intently while I spoke.

"Have you ever seen anything like that before?" Ryze asked with a frown.

I shook my head. "Never. I'm not sure I want to again. I felt like I was standing in someone else's body." I couldn't contain the shudder that passed through me. If something like that were to happen when I was supposed to be killing someone, I may end up being the dead Fae. I didn't much care for that idea.

"Did you get any sense of whose body it was?" Cavan asked. "Thoughts that weren't your own?"

I considered his question, but eventually shook my head again. "No, it was me. Just...not me. I didn't think to look down at myself or anything like that. I'm not sure I was able to. I think I could only look where they were looking. Whoever's body I was in."

"The people you saw didn't see anything out of place?" Cavan asked.

"They were too busy being angry with each other." I shrugged. "But the griffins and the mountains would seem to track with all of this." I gestured towards the maps still lying on the table.

After a moment I added, "There's something else. I didn't get the impression they were the same time-frame. The battlefield on the mountain didn't happen at the same time. I think one was the past and the other the future. Or the present maybe?"

"Let's hope the battlefield was the past," Ryze said. "If that's the future, I'm going to be really, really pissed off."

"That might be the first thing you've said that I agree with," Cavan said. "I suggest we get to Haven-moor now. Take a look at that map before it's too late."

"I think we should take Hycanthe with us," Khala said softly. She sighed and started to explain.

20

KHALA

"I can't believe you *fucking told them*," Hycanthe snarled. Only Jezalyn's hand on her arm kept her from lunging at me. She looked ready to scratch my eyes out.

Perhaps it was the proximity of two High Lords, the Commander of the Winter Court army, the master of assassins, and Dalyth that stopped her. All of them were watching us with varying degrees of interest or amusement. Or annoyance, in Vayne's case.

"I didn't have a choice," I said regretfully. "You put out that wind, didn't you?"

Hycanthe leaned back and glared at me. "I don't know what you—"

"You might as well tell her," Jezalyn said softly, her voice only loud enough for the three of us to hear. "Dalyth was there too."

Hycanthe gave her a glance that bordered on resentful before she exhaled loudly.

"Fine, yes I did. I got a burst of magic and somehow managed to put a bunch of warm air under the wind and force it up. I don't know how I did it, I just did. And then my magic went back to normal after that."

"You're tied to all of this," I told her. "You and Tavian. Ryze and Cavan. Maybe the rest of us too. Do you want to understand what's happening to you?"

"Do I have a choice?" she snapped.

"Of course you do," Ryze said. He stepped over and placed a hand on my shoulder. "You can stay here and let us figure it out, if we can. Or you can come with us and help us. I have a feeling what we find may be enlightening. You might be much more powerful than anyone realises."

She was clearly unsure whether she liked that idea or not.

I had to remind myself she'd been through the same thing I had, at around the same time. People deal with traumatic events in different ways. The only person she was sure she could trust was Jezalyn.

She'd trusted me enough to tell me about her magic and I'd betrayed that. I regretted hurting her, but not being forthcoming.

Cavan was right, keeping secrets was getting us nowhere. We had to be open with each other and work together to figure this out. The alternative was waiting for Hycanthe to speak out for herself, or asking Jezalyn to order her. I'd rather Hycanthe hated me than herself or her alpha.

"Aren't you at least a little bit curious about what we'll find?" Ryze asked. "Lost courts, forgotten magic." He grinned like a little boy.

"What if they don't want to be found?" Hycanthe asked. "What if the wind and that lightning bolt, or whatever it was, was a warning to stay the hells away?"

"Taking aim at my court isn't the best way to warn me off," Ryze said. "On the other hand, it's a really good way to *piss* me off. Either way, we're going. You can come with us, or you can stay here with Dalyth. Or you can go back to the Summer Court. Perhaps Cavan will lock you in the atrium again."

Cavan grimaced, but didn't rise to the bait. Evidently a hundred was enough times to say he only did it for our own good.

Hycanthe and Jezalyn stepped back and spoke in whispers for a minute or two. Finally, Jezalyn stepped forward.

"We're coming with you. But no matter what happens, Hycanthe and I stay together."

"I wouldn't have it any other way," Ryze said. He nodded and turned to Cavan. "You know Havenmoor better than I do. Will you make the portal?"

Cavan nodded. "I thought you'd never ask."

"I didn't want to," Ryze admitted, eyes twinkling. "But here we are." He spread his hands out to either side.

Cavan shook his head but half closed his eyes and placed his palms outward in the air. Where Ryze's portals looked like ice, his looked like fire.

I expected heat to radiate from it, but it was the same temperature as the air in the courtyard. Still, stepping through it was tentative at best. I half-expected to be roasted alive.

Ryze took my hand and walked through with me.

"Disconcerting, isn't it?" He looked up at the—was it a ceiling?—above us. "Walking through ice and snow makes more sense than walking through fire."

"I find them both disconcerting," I admitted. "Is that why mine won't stay open? Because walking through portals freaks me the fuck out?"

He laughed and pulled me closer, to tuck me to his side. "Possibly but probably not. The first time I went through one I made, I felt the same way, and it stayed open."

"It's just me then," I said with a sigh.

"I don't think it's just you," he said. "No more than it's Hycanthe's fault her magic isn't strong except at certain times. And Tavian seeing visions? Probably not a coincidence either. I don't know what any of it means yet. Hopefully we can get some answers."

"Hopefully," I agreed.

We stepped out into a stand of trees. Was it the same forest we'd spent the night when we ran from Dalyth and Cavan's Fae? That seemed like years ago now. Being here in their company was more than a little strange. Not until my feet were on the leafy ground did I realise I'd expected armed Fae to still be here waiting to attack.

In spite of everything Cavan said, trust was thinner than the layer of leaves under my boots.

Cavan closed the portal behind us and glanced around. "I see no sign anyone knows we're here, but us."

"Keep your eyes open for portals in the sky," Ryze instructed. "Or stray griffins."

"Or dragons," Tavian said teasingly.

"At this point, if a dragon appeared, I'm not sure how surprised I'd be," Ryze said wryly.

"Things certainly couldn't get stranger," Cavan said. "Who could have guessed you and I might be civil to each other for more than a minute or two?" Before Ryze could respond, he added, "Don't get too used to it."

"I wouldn't dream of it," Ryze told him. "Are we

going to stand here talking, or are we going to Havenmoor?"

Cavan responded with a curt nod and started away to the north.

Tavian slipped over next to me. "Can you feel Zared?"

I'd been putting off feeling down the bond until now, scared of what I might find. While Tavian held my hand, I reached out.

"He's close," I whispered. "He can't be more than a kilometre or two away."

He seemed tired and angry. What was it that had him so upset? He felt like he was ready to punch someone. Could he feel me too? Should I send nice thoughts, or stay out of the bond?

I didn't know how he'd react to feeling anything from me. He might have felt me all along, and he might not. Better to wait until I saw him face to face.

Tavian squeezed my hand. "I still haven't ruled out stabbing Dalyth for messing with his memories." He looked ahead to where she walked a few steps behind Cavan.

"Me either," I said. She looked like she enjoyed it at the time. She seemed to take pleasure in the suffering of others. Pleasure that went way beyond doing what she was ordered to do.

I still hadn't resolved the fact Cavan was the one

who told her to do it. Regardless of his reasons, it was difficult to forgive and impossible to forget.

Unless Dalyth made me forget.

"We may need her someday," Ryze said. He walked on the other side of me. "Her magic anyway. She seems to be the only one who understands how yours works."

"Did you just admit you don't know something?" Cavan asked over his shoulder.

"Yes, but you don't know it either," Ryze retorted. "Mixing magic has always been complicated."

"Winter Court usually only breeds with Winter Court?" I asked.

"Not so much that," Ryze said slowly. "Usually if Fae from different courts breed, the offspring have one kind of magic or the other. Cases like yours are rare and special."

"How do spring and autumn magic work then?" I asked. "Isn't it a combination of hot and cold too?"

"Not really," Ryze said. "Spring magic is the magic of birth, rebirth and growth. Autumn magic is the magic of—not death exactly. Change, endings. Clearing out of old things to make way for the new. If summer magic can raze a field to the ground, autumn magic can turn the dirt, air it out to plant new seeds. It's good for cleansing things too."

"Nothing gets blood out of clothes like autumn magic does," Tavian said.

"That's good to know." I gave him the side eye.

"You never know when something like that will come in handy," he told me unapologetically.

"I suppose not," I agreed.

We moved quietly through the trees. I kept half an eye on the ground in front of me and half of my attention on the bond. The other three around me were comforting, but I couldn't help but focus on Zared. Every step drew me closer to Havenmoor. Closer to him.

"Are we going to walk into Havenmoor looking like this?" Hycanthe asked.

"You have another suggestion?" Dalyth asked, her tone scathing. "At some point, you're going to have to accept you're Fae now. The sooner you do that, the better."

Hycanthe stewed on that for a minute or two. "You don't think a bunch of Fae walking into Havenmoor won't go unnoticed?"

"They'll notice," Cavan said. "They've seen Dalyth and I there before, along with some of my guards. Not usually in these numbers, but I wouldn't be concerned. It's nothing we can't deal with if they give us any trouble."

"You're going to march into Havenmoor and start killing people?" Hycanthe asked in disbelief.

"There's no need for anyone to die," Cavan told her.

"Even your magic is strong enough to deal with anyone throwing stones or insults." Dalyth smiled at her sarcastically.

One minute Dalyth was standing there looking smug as fuck, the next minute she was flying through the air. She slammed into the trunk of a tree and dangled there, halfway off the ground, face red with annoyance.

"My magic is strong enough for that," Hycanthe said. Now who was looking smug?

"Put her down," Cavan said wearily.

"Where's the hurry?" Ryze asked. "I don't know about the rest of you, but I like her like that. It's nothing she doesn't deserve."

"Fuck off," Dalyth snarled. "Let me down."

She barely finished talking when she was struck in the centre of her chest. Her eyes widened. She opened her mouth to scream. No sound came out before she burst into flame.

"Fuck!" Ryze raised his hands and half a blizzard of snow roared out from the air. Where it met fire, it sizzled. The flames died out in moments.

Even before the smoke and steam cleared, the smell of roasting meat told me it was too late. Dalyth was nothing more than a blackened corpse, now lying at the base of the tree.

"Oh my gods." Hycanthe took several steps back

before Jezalyn managed to grab her. "I didn't mean to... Oh gods."

"It wasn't you," Vayne said. He was looking at the sky over her shoulder. He shook his head. "It opened and closed so quick, I almost missed it."

"Another portal," Ryze said. He was staring at Dalyth's remains.

I turned to stare at Tavian. He seemed to be frozen on the spot, like he was in the library. There, but at the same time not there.

21

———————

KHALA

"Ryze," I said, to get his attention.

"What is it?" He too turned and saw Tavian. "Shit." He stepped over closer to the assassin master. Put a hand on his cheek. "He's colder than ice. Tavian? Tave?"

Tavian blinked a couple of times and shook his head. "Sorry, I was..."

"Let's sit you down." Ryze led him over to a tree and helped him to the ground. "What did you see?"

Tavian's eyes were glazed. "The same Fae as last time. They were talking to someone. I couldn't see who. It was dark. I wasn't supposed to be watching."

I crouched beside him. "What were they talking about?"

He shook his head slowly. "I have no idea. I could

only hear a word or two. It sounded like they were arguing. Then the woman, Yala, she saw me."

"The person whose body you were in?" I asked.

He frowned. "No. She saw *me*. I don't know how. She looked shocked. She started to point to me, and then... I was back here." He looked around. Caught sight of the burnt mess on the ground. "What... Who?"

"Dalyth." Ryze sat down next to him. "Vayne saw another portal open and close. Something came out of it and hit her."

His gaze flicked towards Hycanthe and back again. "Where was she each time?"

I thought back for a moment. "The first time, I don't know. She was with Jezalyn. The second time, she was training with Dalyth."

I suspected Hycanthe had something to do with this, but not to this extent. Whatever 'this extent' was. To me, it seemed like she was stuck right in the middle of it. A place she clearly didn't want to be any more than I did.

"And the third time, Dalyth ended up dead," Ryze said thoughtfully. "And Tave keeps eavesdropping on strange Fae."

"Not on purpose," Tavian protested. "If it's all the same to you, I'd rather not do that again." His wide mouth twisted to the side like he tasted something unpleasant.

"Do you think Hycanthe did this somehow?" I whispered. Hycanthe wasn't my favourite person ever, but I couldn't really imagine her attacking people with anything but her words.

"Not purposefully," Ryze said. "At least, I don't think so." He looked over to Cavan and jerked his head to indicate that he should join us.

Both he and Vayne crouched down beside us.

"You're the closest thing to an expert in Summer Court magic," Ryze started.

Cavan raised his eyebrows, but didn't say anything. He gestured for Ryze to continue.

"Can you pin someone to a tree, open a portal, aim a blast of fire and actually hit the target, all at the same time?"

"At any other time, I'd make the claim I could," Cavan replied easily.

"So, no," Vayne said.

"No," Cavan agreed. "I could pin someone to a tree and make a portal at the same time, or do the other two, but not all of it at once. If you're volunteering, I could demonstrate." He smiled sarcastically.

"Only if I get to pin you to a tree afterward," Ryze said dryly.

Tavian made a choking sound in the back of his throat.

I had to bite my lip to keep myself from smiling.

Ryze sighed exaggeratedly. "Do your omegas have filthy minds too?" he asked Cavan.

Cavan grinned and glanced at me. "I hope so."

"There's no one to find you if I kill you and bury you out here," Ryze growled.

"You'd have to get past my guards first," Cavan pointed out.

"Our guard contingents are evenly matched," Ryze said. "But I have Vayne, which tips the odds in my favour."

"As fascinating as this conversation is," Vayne said, "I'd like to be somewhere not so open if whoever, or whatever, killed Dalyth decides to try again."

"It's good to see someone from the Winter Court has some sense," Cavan said. "I was starting to wonder." He gave me a look that suggested he didn't consider me part of the Winter Court. Presumably because of my mother, he thought of me as a Summer Court Fae. That was a conversation for another day.

He stood and offered me his hand.

I took it and stood, but released it the moment I was upright. Partly because I didn't want to create more conflict, and partly because the heat his touch sent through me made me want to pin him to a tree myself. That wouldn't go unnoticed.

"I have sense," Tavian protested. He pushed himself to his feet. "Right now my sense of smell is almost overwhelmed by the intoxicating scent of alphas. Maybe you can relax a little." He nodded toward Jezalyn to include her too.

Now he mentioned it, the scent was strong. Two alphas competing with each other and one protecting her omega. My own scent flared in response.

Ryze groaned. "Let's get out of here before we end up with an impromptu orgy in the middle of the forest." He adjusted the front of his pants.

"You say *impromptu orgy* like it's a bad thing," Tavian said.

"It's the middle of the forest thing that would be a bad thing," Ryze told him. "And as Vayne reminded us, we are somewhat out in the open."

"Yes we are," Cavan said in a way that made us all look at him. "Unless something has taken place that we're not aware of, then this always happens outside."

"And from the sky," Vayne added. "All the more reason to get inside."

Cavan nodded and turned to Dalyth's remains. He instructed a couple of his guards to remove her head and pack it carefully, then incinerate the rest of her. His expression was tight. Not exactly grief. More like annoyance with a dose of caution. What happened to her could have happened to any of us.

I made a note not to get in Hycanthe's way. Right now, she was standing with Jezalyn's arms around her, staring at what was left of Dalyth. Her eyes were wide and glossy. If somehow she did this, she definitely didn't do it on purpose.

I stepped over to them. "Are you all right?" I asked as gently as I could.

"What do you think?" Hycanthe asked. She exhaled a ragged breath. "I'm sorry. I just..."

"Khala understands," Jezalyn said. "We all know it wasn't you." She looked over at me meaningfully.

I wasn't sure we did know that, but I nodded anyway. "Of course we do," I said. "Whoever is on the other side of the portal took advantage of the moment. That's all. Dalyth was being obnoxious."

She deserved to get thrown against a tree, but did she deserve to die like that? I didn't have the answer. Or maybe I did and didn't want to admit to being bloodthirsty. After what she did to Zared, I couldn't bring myself to regret her death.

"Did your magic get stronger again?" I asked.

"I felt like I could have ripped the tree out by its roots," Hycanthe said. "I almost did, and then... What hit her? It looked like lightning."

"Lightning does seem to be their method," I said. "Lightning and wind." And strange visions of unknown Fae.

"You think the Court of Shadows is responsible, don't you?" Jezalyn asked.

I closed my eyes for a moment and tried to shut out the chopping sound as Dalyth's head was removed from her shoulders by a sword.

"Cavan thinks it is," I said finally. "I don't think the rest of us know what to believe. They'd have to exist, for one thing. For another, they'd have to have a grudge against one of us. For all we know, they were after Dalyth and now it will stop."

"I wish I could believe that," Jezalyn said.

Hycanthe hummed her agreement.

I didn't blame them. I wished I believed it too.

"Let's go," Cavan said when Dalyth's head was suitably wrapped and placed inside one of the guard's packs. The idea of carrying that around made me want to vomit.

The Fae method of preserving skulls was something else I'd have to get used to.

I remembered the line in the song about rows of skulls and wondered if somehow that had something to do with any of this. A pathway of the dead sounded nasty as fuck. Then again, opening portals and firing at people was also nasty as fuck.

"What are you thinking?" Ryze was in front of me, looking at me intently.

"I was thinking life as a Silent Maiden was a lot simpler than this," I said. "The worst thing we had to worry about was getting caught putting salt in the sugar containers. Or whether the cute priest would notice me."

He smiled and kissed my nose. "I know they would have noticed you. Although, if we see any of them at Havenmoor, let me know. I'll have Tave poke their eyes out."

I jabbed him in the side with my elbow. He grabbed my arm and pulled me in for a deeper kiss. We broke off when Vayne cleared his throat behind us.

"I don't think Cavan will leave without Khala, but he would totally leave without the great Lord Ryzellius."

Ryze waved Vayne away. "We'll catch up."

I laughed, grabbed Ryze's hand and pulled him behind me. "We all agreed we don't want to be out in the open. Let's get to Havenmoor."

He pouted, but let me drag him along.

As much as I liked the idea of being sidetracked and pinned to a tree, I needed to see Zared. I needed to know he was all right and could live his life without us. If I never saw him again, I'd have this. I could settle my mind, if not my heart.

We wound our way through the forest, moving carefully. We all glanced at the sky every few moments, always on alert for anything weird. Any strange sound, smell or sensation or sight.

Of course, that had me jumping at rustling from the bushes, or a bird soaring overhead.

One of the guards stepped on a twig, which cracked loudly, making us all jump.

If Jezalyn hadn't stopped Hycanthe, he might have ended up pinned to a tree, she was so startled.

By the time we reached the edge of the trees, we were all as twitchy as fuck.

"I think it would be a good idea if we stay close together," Cavan said.

"All the better to keep an eye on you," Ryze told him.

Cavan gave him a rude gesture with his middle finger, which for some reason made Tavian giggle.

"Maybe we can not argue amongst ourselves for a while," I suggested. "If we stay close together, we can help keep each other safe."

"Exactly," Cavan said, giving Ryze a long look.

Ryze nodded. "No one get complacent." He pulled me closer to him. "Keep your magic ready, in case you need it. You too, Hycanthe. If they come at us again with wind, we'll need all the heat we can get. I'll be ready with a shield of ice if they throw lightning at us."

"That sounds like a solid plan to me," Vayne said. He stepped in closer to the rest of us. Not having any magic, he must have felt slightly vulnerable. Not that he'd ever admit to it.

"Of course it is," Ryze said. He gave Vayne a cocky smile, but it wasn't as cocky as usual. He couldn't know what might come at us, if anything.

We walked for a few minutes until we found the road.

"Havenmoor is half a kilometre away, approximately," Cavan said. "I would have opened a portal closer, but the humans tend to... How do I put it? Shoot arrows first and ask questions later. Walking in won't scare them so much."

"Have you had to dodge arrows often?" Ryze asked him.

"More than I'd like to admit," Cavan said. "Humans are a twitchy bunch at best."

"And at worst?" I asked. I was half-human after all.

"At worst, they'll happily kill any Fae they see, just for sport. They won't stop to see if they recognise you.Were they to do that, they may suspect we did something to you to make you one of us."

Tavian grinned. "We did do something to her. I think she liked it."

I felt a tug on the bond and froze. "It's Zared."

22

KHALA

"Where?" Ryze asked.

"Not far," I replied. "Up ahead. But he's upset, excited, angry. He's coming this way. I think they know we're here."

"Are you ready to dodge more arrows?" Ryze asked Cavan.

"If I have to," Cavan said. "It would be better to slip around them. Stay out of their way. We can get into Havenmoor, look at the temple and get back out again."

Ryze considered for a moment, then nodded. "Everyone off the road. We'll go through the bushes." He waved us ahead of him.

I gave him a pleading look, but he waved me off too.

"You heard what Cavan said. They won't look twice

at any of us, including you. That bond might be confusing the hells out of him."

Reluctantly, I followed the others into the thick bushes, and kept low, close to Tavian.

"It'll be all right," he whispered.

I didn't know what he was basing that on, because right now it didn't feel all right.

"The smoke was coming from around here," a voice said.

Zared.

"It might be nothing," another voice said.

"I'm telling you, Ianic, there's something fucked as hells going on," Zared insisted. "It wasn't a random event. I can't explain how I know, but I know."

He stopped in front of the bushes. He was close enough to touch. Close enough to smell his cedar scent. He turned his face.

I'd swear he looked right at me.

"I don't see anything," Ianic said. "It was probably nothing more nefarious than a hunter cooking a rabbit."

"You're right," Zared said a bit too quickly. "I'm sure it was nothing. Let's get back to the temple. Tyla is probably waiting for you to fuck her mouth again."

Ianic chuckled. "She does like being on her knees."

I stiffened at the way they were talking about my

friend. Not because I was ashamed of anything she did with Ianic, or anyone else, but he didn't seem to have much respect for her.

"You go on ahead," Zared said. "I'm going to take a piss."

"All right. I don't want to keep her and her mouth waiting." Ianic's footsteps crunched away down the road.

I held my breath while Zared stepped in front of the bush again.

"All right, you can come out and explain what the fuck is going on," he snarled.

"We're right here with you," Tavian whispered.

At the same time, Ryze gestured for everyone else to stay out of sight. He sent reassuring thoughts through the bond and pulled his bow off his back. He readied an arrow, then nodded to me.

Hopefully he wouldn't feel the need to use it. If he hurt Zared...

I put my hands in the air to either side of me and slowly stood.

"Hello." The smile I gave him was forced at best. Tentative in the face of his expression.

Zared stared at me with utter confusion. He squinted. Recognition, then shock crossed his features.

He shook his head and took a few steps back.

"What the fuck? I thought I could feel Khala. You look like her, but..." He reached a hand back and gripped the hilt of his sword.

"I am Khala," I said evenly. "I look a little bit different, that's all. It's still me. Your...your friend."

Dalyth said she removed his memories from after the attack on the caravan. We were only friends back then, although he'd wanted more. So had I, but I hadn't wanted to ruin things between us.

"The hells you are," he snapped. "What did you do to her? Why can I feel you? What did you do to me?" He looked at me with such fear and loathing, like I was some kind of monster.

I was starting to think I should have tried harder to stay away from him.

"I am Khala," I insisted. I took a step toward him. Then another.

He drew his sword and held it out in front of him, a hand away from my throat.

"Don't come any closer. I don't know who you are or what you've done, but you're not her. She's not *Fae*." He spat the word like he was disgusted.

I stopped still. "What do you remember of her? When did you see her last?"

He frowned. "I can't—"

"When did you see her last?" I insisted. If I knew that, I'd have some idea how much Dalyth took from him. Right now, she was lucky she was dead, because if she wasn't I'd kill her for this.

"Right after she had her choker taken off by that Fae. Did she do this? Khala was supposed to go to Havenmoor. Then... She was supposed to go somewhere else. Where is she?" His hands trembled slightly. The blade dipped and weaved in front of me.

"She's safe." I put up a hand to push the blade away, but he managed to hold it steady again.

"I don't believe you," he said. "What did you do to her?" He sounded so devastated a piece of my heart broke.

"You're right, that Fae woman did something. She wanted you to forget Khala. She changed your memories, but she's dead now. She won't be able to do the same thing to anyone else."

"Why would she do that?" he demanded.

"Because she was a sadistic bitch." That was accurate, if not entirely truthful. "She got pleasure out of messing with humans. I came here to see what damage she'd done. I'm sorry she did this to you. You didn't deserve this."

His mouth twisted. "She's dead?"

"Yes. That smoke you saw? That was her. She's been dealt with." I felt like a real Fae now, skirting around the truth while not lying.

I tentatively raised my hand and pushed the blade to the side.

"I know it's hard to believe anything I say, but Khala is fine. She... She wishes she could see you again. She hates what Dalyth did to you." I blinked back tears. If he couldn't accept I was me, then maybe this would give him what he needed. A final close of the door between us. A twist of the key in the lock.

"Why can I feel you?" he asked in a rough whisper. He dropped the sword down until the point almost touched the road. "Why do you feel like her?" His voice was choked with emotion.

All I could think to say was, "So I could find you. To make sure you're all right after what was done to you. It's a thing Fae can do. Are you all right?" I hated lying to him, but if the truth was too hard for him to take, I had no other choice.

He looked down at his sword for a minute or two, then put it back in its sheath.

"Of course I'm all right. It takes more than one Fae bitch to fuck with me."

That was the Zared I knew.

I forced a smile. "Of course it does. I'm glad you're doing well. I should let you go on your way. I have to make another stop before I return home. A visit to the Temple in Havenmoor. I have business there. An offering to make." He wouldn't refuse to let me go if I had a gift for the gods. The Fae visited rarely, but were always generous when they did. I overheard Geralda mention the fact once. Something about fine wine and a bag of money. Recompense for taking care of the maidens for the Summer Court, perhaps?

"That's where I'm going," he said reluctantly. "I can show you if you want."

"I'd appreciate that," I said graciously.

Without thinking, I reached out and touched his hand.

He jerked away as if my touch stung his skin.

Froze.

He clapped his hands to either side of his head and felt to his knees in the dirt. A jolt of pure agony surged through the bond.

"Shit, Zared!" I dropped down beside him and grabbed him before he could topple.

Ryze and Tavian darted out from behind the bushes and helped me lower him until he lay on the ground. His legs kicking, body writhing.

"Gods, what did I do?" His pain was so intense I swear I felt it too.

"Stop panicking," Cavan ordered as he too stepped out of the bushes. "You have the magic to ease his pain."

"I'm not going to—" I started.

"I'm not suggesting you kill him," Cavan snapped. "Focus."

Without knowing what I was doing, I placed my hands on either side of Zared's face, beside his. I pushed a combination of numbing cold and soothing warmth into him. That was when I found it.

"She didn't change his memories," I said absently. "There's a block. If I move it, will it kill him?"

"If you don't, this may kill him," Ryze said. I felt a sliver of his cold magic curl around mine. A moment later, Cavan added a dash of warmth.

"We've got him," Ryze said. "We'll try to keep the pain at bay while you deal with the block."

Zared still writhed, but the agony wasn't quite so bad.

I sucked in a breath. Cavan's order not to panic kept me from losing it completely.

I focused my attention and my magic on the block in Zared's mind. It felt like a wall made of pure thought. Like Dalyth created an idea and pushed it into place there.

Ideas, once settled into the mind, were always difficult to shift. This one was no different. It clung to him stubbornly even while he rejected it.

I closed my eyes and sent my own thoughts down the bond.

I am Khala. I was transformed into a Fae. I was always part Fae. You know all of this, you were there. I'm an omega. I went through heat and changed. You were there for that too. You're part of my pack. You were always meant to be part of my pack.

The block started to disintegrate, bit by bit. It clung on stubbornly, tendrils trying to dig invisible claws into Zared's mind. I teased away each one, until only one large piece remained. One particularly stubborn section. I poked at it with my magic.

Zared arched his back, threw his head back and howled in pain.

"Quickly," someone urged. I didn't know whose voice it was. It might have been Ryze's, or even Tavian.

I had no choice but to reach in and shatter the last piece of the block. For the longest while, it resisted. I growled in the back of my throat and pushed harder. Eventually the shard disintegrated along with the remaining fragments. A heartbeat later, nothing was left.

Zared writhed a couple more times before he finally fell still. His brow was covered with sweat, but his skin was frigid.

"Is he dead?" Hycanthe asked.

I didn't know when she and Jezalyn stepped back onto the road, but they were here now, leaning over us all. Hycanthe looked as worried as I'd ever seen her. Jezalyn clutched her arm.

"No," Ryze said. "But we won't know if he's all right until he's able to speak." He and Cavan both sat back.

I smoothed hair back off Zared's brow. "I shouldn't have come here. I shouldn't have touched him. That must have triggered something. Did Dalyth set booby-traps in people's minds in case things like this happened?"

"If she did, it's a good thing she's dead," Cavan growled. "I certainly didn't ask anything like that of her."

Ryze glanced at him, but turned away. "It's more likely to be the bond. You two being that close together, the bond fought against what Dalyth did. Zared's memories wanted to resurface. Chances are, this would have happened sooner or later anyway. If it happened when we weren't here, he'd be dead."

"He fought to remember me," Tavian said to lighten the mood.

I managed to give him a smile. "Of course he did. You're unforgettable."

"I am, aren't I?" He grinned.

Zared groaned and shifted slightly.

The next thing I knew, I was lying on my back in the dirt, Zared straddling my thighs. I was ready to fight back, but then his mouth slammed down onto mine.

"I think he remembers her," Tavian remarked with a laugh.

Zared's tongue thrust into my mouth. I managed to get my arms around him and opened my mouth so our tongues could tangle.

He tasted so good. The pain was gone from the bond, replaced by hunger. For me. For my body.

He slid his hands up my shirt and over my breasts. My nipples went hard under his palms.

"We can't just—" We were lying on the road in full view of everyone.

"Yes we can," he growled.

"We don't mind," Tavian said.

"I do," Hycanthe said. Because of course she would. I was tempted to fuck him then and there just for that.

"We've been out in the open long enough," Ryze said. "Your cock will have to wait a while longer."

Zared exhaled loudly and pressed his cheek to mine, his stubble scratching my skin. "Fine, but you all have a fuck ton of explaining to do." He rolled off me and helped me to my feet.

"You can start by telling me what the fuck he's doing here." Zared's hand was back on the hilt of his sword, his eyes on Cavan.

"We'll catch you up while we walk to Havenmoor,"

Ryze said. "Wait until you've heard all of that before you run Cavan through."

"Fine." Zared dropped his hand and took hold of mine. We walked side by side and I told him what he missed during the last few days. Including all the reasons why he probably shouldn't stab Cavan.

23

"So this is the shit you get up to when I'm not around," he said. "Lost Fae courts, melting stone and excessive wind. I can't believe I missed watching Dalyth become toast."

"One of the guards has her head in their bag if you want to look." I wrinkled my nose. "I don't recommend it. It's not pretty. Is Tyla all right?"

"She's fit right in at Havenmoor. She thinks you were sent to a temple in Freid or Gerian and that you're content."

"She's happy?" Since we didn't have a bond, there was no reason to expect her mind would fight the block. And if she was happy, there's no reason to remove it, even if she wasn't at risk. She was probably better off not remembering her time in the Summer Court.

"Happier than I was," he said. "I kept feeling like something was missing. The bond tugged at me. I thought I was imagining it. How could I be feeling someone else's emotions? I knew they weren't mine, but they had to be. Only they weren't." A heavy frown sat on his brow.

"No, because they were mine." I squeezed his hand. "What happens now?"

"What do you mean?" His brow uncreased. "This doesn't change anything. We're a pack. It sounds like we have a world to save or some shit. I don't belong in the Temple. But I can show you where that map is. No one will ask any questions about why you're there if I'm there too."

"Maybe the gods planned for this to happen," Tavian said. "It's the kind of fucked up thing they'd do. Mess with Zared so he could help us later."

"That's most fucked up thing I think I've ever heard," I said.

"That's because you're young," Ryze said. "When you get to our age, you will have heard a plethora of stuff way more fucked up than that. Although, that is pretty fucked up."

"As if the gods don't have better things to do," Hycanthe said scathingly.

Zared looked over his shoulder at her. "It's nice to see you haven't changed. Still as sweet as vinegar."

She stuck her middle finger up at him. "You're still annoying."

He turned to me. "You must have been really happy to see she was one of the maidens who transformed too."

I shrugged. "We have to learn to get along at some point."

"At least Hycanthe and I transformed together," Jezalyn said. "It would have been really awkward otherwise."

"Not necessarily," Tavian said. "You still would have been alpha and omega. Call me a romantic, but I think you would have ended up together anyway."

Jezalyn gave Hycanthe each other a loving look. "That's true. If I wasn't an alpha, it might have been difficult, but all I want is what's best for her." She leaned over to kiss Hycanthe's cheek.

Zared grimaced. "There's no accounting for taste."

I socked him lightly on the arm. "Be nice. Hycanthe is trying to save the world too."

"Exactly," Hycanthe said, looking smug. "All you're doing is being a distraction."

"He's an attractive distraction," Tavian said. "I, for one, am glad he's back with us." He didn't break his stride to put an arm around Zared and give him a hug.

"We're all glad," Ryze said. He gave Zared a warm

smile. "Even though the last time I saw you, you would have happily cut my throat."

"The last time I saw you, you were happy to let Khala go into his palace." Zared jerked a thumb towards Cavan. "You were engineering a plan to have her get taken."

"As I recall, I suggested you leave Garial," Ryze said. "You insisted on staying. You were supposed to hide, remember?"

"You misjudged," Zared said.

"At least I didn't have him executed," Cavan pointed out.

"We're very grateful for that," I told him.

"You did all of that to help Hycanthe and me?" Jezalyn asked.

"They did all of that not knowing it was you and me," Hycanthe said. She glanced over to me. "Would you have bothered if you knew?"

"It didn't matter who it was," I said firmly. "I thought my sisters were at risk and I wanted to get you out, whoever you were."

Hycanthe looked disbelieving, but Jezalyn patted her arm and whispered in her ear. Soothing words, presumably, because Hycanthe backed down and fell quiet.

"Imagine all the hassle that could have been

avoided if more communication took place," Cavan said.

"You're never going to get past that, are you?" Ryze asked.

"Twenty years of trying to tell you there's a risk that might destroy our courts? No, probably not."

"In that case, if you're wrong, I get to remind you every chance I get," Ryze told him.

"Since you're also walking on the road to Havenmoor, to look at a map, I'd suggest you're as wrong about this as I am," Cavan said. "At this point, we're equally invested."

"Maybe I'm just humouring you," Ryze said.

"I'd literally pay money to see them kiss each other," Tavian said with a groan.

Ryze and Cavan both turned to give him a look.

Tavian shrugged. "What? The sexual tension around here is hotter than that melted building."

Cavan and Ryze shared a look.

Ryze grimaced. "It is not sexual tension between me and him. It's a genuine, carefully cultivated dislike. Honed by years of him being an asshole."

"I was about to say exactly the same thing," Cavan said. "Although, I was going to say stubborn, ignorant asshole."

"I might be stubborn, but I'm not ignorant," Ryze protested. "We have years of mistrust between us. It's a centuries' old pattern. I had no reason to think anything changed."

"Except me sending envoys to try to get you to listen," Cavan snapped.

"See, sexual tension." Tavian sighed.

Ryze stopped in the middle of the road. "What envoys? None ever came from you talking about any of this."

"Because you didn't listen—" Cavan stopped too.

The only sound was the wind in the trees and the crunch of the guards' footsteps until they caught up with us.

"Not one word," Ryze said. "The Winter Court never got a word about any part of this from you or from anyone else. The first I heard of any of it were rumours about Silent Maidens being taken to the Summer Court, and the weather being screwed with. That was all relatively recent."

"They never returned." Cavan closed his eyes tight. He exhaled loudly out his nose, like an angry bull. "They never *arrived*."

His words fell in silence that lingered for a couple of minutes while we all absorbed the meaning and the implications.

"Who thinks they didn't make it past the Autumn Court?" Tavian raised his hand.

I raised mine as well. Ryze raised his, but Zared shrugged.

"Whether it's Harel or some other faction, someone has been working against us for a long time. Sowing the seeds of division between us. And we let them grow." Cavan opened his eyes. "Khala, what was it you said? Something about building bridges and getting over things."

"I was talking about you and my mother, but this is a good example too," I said. "We're all on the same side here. We don't have to like each other, but we need to stop being divided. That might even include Harel." I added that grudgingly because I really wanted to punch him in the face.

Cavan sighed and ducked his head for a moment before looking back up again. His generous mouth was pressed in a tight line.

"Let's get a look at this map first," he said. "Then we can make a plan."

"I can agree with that," Ryze said. "Although I have the horrible feeling that means going into the mist." He seemed more resigned when he talked about it now.

"It means whatever it means," Cavan said. "I think you all realise I'll do whatever it takes to stop our courts from being destroyed. Even if that means going into the mist and never coming back."

Ryze opened his mouth, probably to say something sarcastic, but he closed it again and nodded.

"You're right. I'll do whatever it takes to keep the Winter Court safe too. Even if I have to be nice to Harel."

"I'll tolerate him," Tavian said. "I don't promise to be nice."

"Me either," I agreed. I wouldn't rule out the possibility of telling him to fuck off again, if I had to. Especially if he called me names.

"I didn't see much of him and I also don't promise to be nice," Zared said. "He seemed like a prick to me."

"He definitely is," Ryze agreed. He resumed walking, but his expression was troubled.

I had a feeling realising Cavan tried so hard to warn him was a hit to his ego. He was so certain Cavan couldn't be trusted. That he was the one causing all the trouble in the first place. And now, it seemed he was very much wrong. Or at least misguided. He couldn't have known those envoys were sent and went missing, or were killed.

I stepped close enough to Tavian that I could speak low and not be overheard.

"Those assassins who went missing in the Summer Court, who were they sent to assassinate?"

Tavian glanced over at me. His apple and cinnamon scent was a comfort I needed amidst the turmoil and chaos. He was like a warm hug even when he didn't have his arms around me. Sometimes it was hard to remember he had anything to do with assassins at all. He seemed more likely to be in a bakery making cakes and tasty pies.

Instead, he could cut a person's throat without them knowing he was even there. Should that be as hot as it was? Possibly not, but it was anyway.

"Mostly business people who cheated on their business partners. Why?"

"Are you sure they disappeared and weren't working for someone else?" I asked. "Is there any chance they were keeping an eye out for any envoys, taking care of them and then slipping away?"

"It's not impossible," he agreed after a minute or two of thought. "Assassins tend to be loyal, but that doesn't necessarily mean they were loyal to me. If that's the case, they were in our midst for a long time. Creating discord and division and watching us."

"How long was Illaria in the Winter Court?"

"Years," it was Vayne who replied. He'd veered close enough to us to hear the last question. "I saw her there watching training at least once a week for years. I never considered her a threat."

"Whatever's going on, they're playing a long game," I said. A game that started before I was even born.

When would it end?

24

KHALA

The temple at Havenmoor was twice as large as the one in Ebonfalls. Weathered pale stone stood tall. Carvings around the doors had long since lost their definition. They might have once been flowers and vines, or random patterns. I couldn't tell.

In spite of that, everything was in a good state of repair. None of the stones were cracked. The mortar in the gaps seemed relatively new.

The biggest difference was the sound. Not just because my Fae hearing was better, but because priests, priestesses and those in training moved around, talking and laughing amongst themselves. It was a far cry from the Silent Maidens.

Until they noticed us.

Then they stopped to stare or hurried on their way.

"No arrows yet," Ryze remarked.

"Yet," Vayne said ominously.

"Give them time," Cavan added.

"They won't do anything," Zared assured them. "You're here with me."

"That doesn't fill any of us with as much confidence as you want it to," Hycanthe told him.

"If you prefer, I can tell them you forced me to bring you here." He pretended to genuinely consider the idea.

"How about you don't?" Vayne growled. "If you're sticking with us, you're still serving under me." He pointed a finger at Tavian before the Master of Assassins could comment on the potential innuendo.

Tavian raised his hands and grinned with mock innocence. "I wasn't going to say a word."

"Bullshit." Vayne lowered his hand. "We know you better than that."

"Where is this map?" Ryze was unusually tense. He didn't stop to banter with the others. His attention seemed to be everywhere at once.

I felt his high alert through the bond. Not alert against anything in particular, just on guard.

"This way." Zared looked relieved to change the subject.

I reminded myself he still hadn't gotten used to the whole idea of the Fae in the first place, much less his attraction to Tavian or any other man. That was something none of us would push, although Tavian would flirt. That was him. Unapologetically so. It was one of the things I adored about him.

We followed Zared through a side door, and into the cool interior. The dimly lit passageway was a stark contrast to the bright sunshine outside. Some people might have found it enclosing, but I found it comforting. Not just because of the attacks, but because it felt cozy.

As Tavian would say, it's an omega thing. We liked to feel safe and snug.

The layout of the temple was familiar. The passageway led to a wide hall for receiving gifts intended for the gods. That in turn led to a bigger hall, this one for prayers.

Several people knelt on the floor, heads down. None looked up as we walked past as silently as we could.

"Back here," Zared said softly. He opened the door to another room at the rear of the temple.

Another room for prayer, this one looked older than the rest of the temple. The stone was more worn, a faded rug on the floor. Cobwebs hung from the ceiling here or there.

Cavan stepped past Zared, and raised his hand. What looked like flame flickered over his palm and fingers, illuminating the wall.

I stared for a moment before realising I could do the same thing. I raised my hand and called on the magic. Instead of the warm, yellow-orange flame, mine was a silvery-white, like a cross between ice and fire. It lit up the wall where Cavan's didn't reach.

"Nice," he told me. "You're learning."

"Of course she is," Ryze said. "Khala is smart and competent. And gorgeous." He stepped into the light of my magic, kissed my mouth, then moved aside to look at the map.

"I noticed all of those things," Cavan told him, although most of his attention seemed to be on the wall in front of him. "Have you got that transcript and sketch?"

"I do." Tavian pulled the paper out of his pocket and unfolded it. He held it up in front of the wall, below the mountain range so we could all see.

"Havenmoor is down here." Zared pointed. "That's Ebonfalls. They look really close together here." They were less than a fingertip apart.

"Freid and Gerian are there," Cavan gestured. "Seasonal courts here, here, here, and there. Natanya is there."

"The mists are around here." Ryze traced a circle around the base of the mountains. An area that must have been at least fifty kilometres long.

"What is this?" I leaned in to peer at the area that

was indicated on the paper map. Symbols were carved into the wall.

At first I didn't recognise them. It took me a moment to realise. "Those look like Silent Maiden hand signals."

"What does it say?" Ryze asked.

Tavian leaned in and squinted. "It says something about death. Death awaits... Death..." He looked over his shoulder at me.

"The closest I can interpret is death seeks," I said. "Death is looking. Looking for... An end? Or a beginning. Those two are similar, but neither are quite right."

I made the signs with my hands, but shook my head. "Either they wanted it to mean both, or the meaning has changed over time."

I looked at the next line. "Bone in rows. The song talks about skulls in rows."

"Anything about trees?" Ryze asked.

"The... Plant... Bush? That could be tree. The tree has answers or accepts the sacrifice. To open a... Window is the closest interpretation. To open a window, one must remain behind. Two who are one. Or one who will give everything." I shook my head. "That's about as much sense as it makes."

"So feed someone to the tree and get answers?" Tavian asked, possibly facetiously.

"The hells kind of tree is that?" Vayne asked.

"I'm going to go out on a limb here and suggest it's a hungry tree," Tavian said. "Pun not intended."

"That pun was totally fucking intended," Vayne told him.

Tavian grinned.

"Like I said before, I'm new to this Fae stuff, but I've never heard of a hungry tree," I said. "Hungry people, hungry animals—"

"Hungry pussies," Ryze said.

I snorted softly. "But never a hungry tree. I'm guessing they don't mean fertiliser." I looked around at them all.

"Why are they using hand symbols as a language?" Hycanthe frowned.

"It might be the language that came first and was turned into hand symbols," Ryze suggested.

"Or they did it so only a... select few could read it," Cavan said.

"You were going to say handful, weren't you?" Tavian asked him. "We don't mind puns around here."

Cavan gave him a funny look, then turned his attention back to the map. "There's more symbols down here. That's the pass leading into the mountains. Before Ryze's beloved mist."

"I'd say I can't wait to see the expression on your

face if you go there," Ryze said. "But that shit is so thick, I wouldn't see it anyway."

Cavan ignored him. "Khala, what do these say?"

I had to crouch down to make them out. "Fire, ice, birth, death. A... Junction? Crossroads?" I shook my head. "Where all four meet comes a path." I stood. "I don't know what that means. Do we need someone from each of the seasonal courts?"

"Yes, but it's worse than that," Ryze said. "There's one place where all four courts meet. Neutral ground during times of conflict. Each High Lord, or a representative, has a key."

"It's called Nallis," Cavan said. "It can only be entered with all four keys."

"So we need Harel?" Vayne scowled.

"We don't need Harel, just his key," Ryze said. "Which he's not going to give up, no matter how nicely we ask."

Cavan pressed a finger to his lip. "So we're going to have to figure out how to get it without asking."

"High Lord Cavan, are you suggesting we steal it?" Ryze cocked his head, a faint smile gracing his lips. "I'm absolutely shocked."

"Try to contain it," Cavan told him, his expression deadpan. "Yes, we may have to steal it."

"So you really don't have an alliance with him?"

Vayne asked. "Because it seems to me now would be a good time to have one of those. Or at least fake it."

Cavan's expression didn't change. "I never fake," he said. "I could probably get in the front door of his palace, but beyond that..."

"This would be easier if Harel wasn't an asshole," Ryze said. "But if there is a pathway through Nallis that means not going through the mists, I'll do just about anything to get there."

"Have you been there before?" I asked. "To Nallis, I mean."

"Once," Ryze replied. "There hasn't been a need ever since. I don't remember seeing a tunnel there, but I wasn't looking for one. Unless..."

"Yes, unless," Cavan agreed.

"Don't keep us hanging, unless what?" Tavian asked.

"Nallis has a guardian of sorts. No one really knows what it is, but it lives under the building itself. Every so often, you can feel it moving around. The earth rumbles. If I was going to have a hidden tunnel, that's where it would be."

"I think we should include Harel in this," Tavian said. "He can supply his key and then this guardian can have him for lunch while the rest of us run like hells."

"I can get behind that suggestion," I said.

"Me too," Zared agreed. "So, how do we steal his key?"

"We make a plan," Ryze said.

"Khala and I will go," Cavan said softly. "I can get us in, and keep him distracted. Any of the rest of you would be too suspicious."

"I did tell him to fuck off," I pointed out. I wasn't sure how I felt about any of this.

"But then I punished you and you've learnt your lesson," he said. "He'll believe that I wanted to show you off. To prove that you're beaten."

Ryze snorted.

I was inclined to agree. Pretending to be broken seemed like a stretch, regardless of what was at stake.

"If I have to, I'll order her to behave like she's scared of me, and won't dare to disobey." Cavan gave me a heated look like he wouldn't mind acting out this fantasy.

A sliver of heat went through me and pooled between my legs. I liked when Zared ordered me around. I suspected I'd like it very much if Cavan did it too.

"I hate to say it, but that makes sense," Tavian said. "If you can get both of you in, I sneak in and help where I can. No one would believe Ryze is paying Harel a social call. That puts Vayne out too. And if somehow those attacks have something to do with

Hycanthe, she's better off staying out of sight somewhere."

"You go in, do what you have to do and get out immediately," Ryze told Cavan. "And if you get her killed..."

"I won't get her killed," Cavan said evenly. He closed his hand and the magic light went out. "We should leave first thing in the morning. Zared, is there somewhere we can spend the night?"

"Yes, there are visitors' quarters beside the temple," Zared said. "I'll show you where, but then I'd like some time alone with Khala. There are some things we need to sort out."

After getting his memories back, he probably had at least a million questions. I'd answer them as best I could, although I wasn't sure how much I knew. I didn't know why my touch made the bond push back so hard. I didn't know if it would work on anyone else, bond or no bond. I didn't know if everyone had a block like he did, and I didn't much want to find out. I didn't want to be like Dalyth, violating other people's minds.

Did he feel like I'd violated his? He said he wanted to stay with us, with me, but what if he changed his mind? I hoped like hells he wasn't about to ask me to put the block back. Even if I wanted to, I wasn't sure I knew how.

If he asked me to, I'd try. That was all I could do.

25

KHALA

"If I haven't said it before, I'm sorry you got dragged into all of this in the first place."

I turned to Zared as he closed the door behind us. "We should have been better prepared back in the Summer Court. Or stayed in the Winter Court. Or—"

There was a lot I felt I needed to apologise for. He'd been dragged over the proverbial coals because of me. He could have died. I never would have forgiven myself if he had.

He shrugged. "None of that matters now." He grabbed my wrists and pulled me to him. "Be honest. How much of you coming here was about seeing that map and how much was it about me?" He looked me dead in the eyes.

I met his gaze unwaveringly. "The map was an

excuse to see you. I had no idea touching you could bring back your memories."

His grip on my wrists tightened. "If you knew, would you have touched me?" His pretty hazel eyes searched mine, unashamed desperation burning there.

I knew what he needed to hear. I had to take a few moments to consider the question. I wanted to give him total honesty. He deserved that.

"If it wasn't for the bond, you would have accepted what I told you when I said the human version of me was content," I said slowly. "You would have returned to the temple and that would have been that."

He shook his head, dark hair falling over one eye. "I would have known something was missing. I would have tried to find out where you were. And when I couldn't find you... I couldn't just move on. The gods meant for us to be together. I fully believe that."

"You believe in the gods?" I couldn't help the light tease. "I remember now. Your favourite is the god of jokesters. If he intended for us to be together, then what does that mean?"

Zared grimaced. "It means we make each other laugh?" he ventured.

He closed his eyes and exhaled out his nose before he opened them again. "You didn't answer the question. Would you have touched me?"

I glanced down towards his muscular chest, then

back up again. Gods, he was so handsome it was ridiculous.

"I know people seem to think I'm selfless and caring. I'm not. I'm selfish. So many times I knew I should push you away but I couldn't. I didn't, because I wanted you to be with me. So, yes, I would have touched you if I knew it would make you remember me. I need you. I'm sorry, that probably makes me a total bitch." If he had any sense, he should have run away from me.

Instead, he immediately said, "Not at all. If the situation was reversed, I'd touch you too, in a heartbeat. I always had trouble keeping my hands off you anyway." He raised my wrists, tugging me until our chests met.

"Really?" I teased. "I hadn't noticed."

He grinned, then slammed his mouth down onto mine. His tongue shoved its way between my lips and rammed almost down my throat.

I sucked like it was his cock.

I didn't hear the door open and close, but then Tavian spoke. "Do you mind if I join? I brought a little something."

Zared and I broke apart and turned to the Master of Assassins.

Tavian raised his hand. In his palm he held a bottle of lubricating oil.

I glanced back at Zared. Anything that happened

between him and Tavian had to be his choice. Truthfully, the idea of them together sent wet warmth right between my legs. If they both wanted it, I was one hundred percent here for it.

After what felt like a lifetime of held breaths, Zared finally nodded. "Are you as obedient as Khala?"

Tavian grinned with relief and excitement. "Definitely. Tell us what you want your dutiful omegas to do."

The heat between my legs grew to inferno level. My whole body trembled with anticipation.

Zared rubbed his chin in thought. "Take each other's clothes off." He grabbed a chair from the side of the room, turned it to face the bed and sat down. He leaned back and crossed his knees, one eyebrow raised.

He reminded me a little of Ryze, but now was not the time to vocalise such a comparison.

"You heard the man," Tavian said. He started oh-so slowly unbuttoning my shirt and slid it off my shoulders. When it pooled on the floor, I did the same to him.

He undid my pants and I shimmied out of them, and my panties. I kicked them aside and helped him out of his.

I glanced over to see Zared with his own pants undone, stroking his hand over his own erect cock.

"Lie down on your stomach," Zared said to Tavian. "Your feet are still on the floor."

"Yes sir." Tavian did as he asked. He lay face first, his legs hanging off the end of the bed, legs apart, ass in the air.

Zared grabbed up the lubricating oil and handed it to me. "Prepare his ass for me."

Holy gods, yes please. Just when I thought I couldn't get any hotter and wetter with anticipation, I did.

Surprised by his confidence and eagerness, I took the jar, unscrewed the top and dipped my fingers inside. I warmed it with a bit of magic and eased a finger carefully inside Tavian's rear hole. He was warm and tight. The idea of Zared's cock sliding in there...

"Is this all right?" I asked.

Tavian groaned. "More than all right. Use more fingers to stretch me. Don't be afraid to hurt me. If Ryze can fit in there, your fingers can."

Now there was a mental image to keep a girl warm on a cold winter's night.

I slid in another finger, and another. My body throbbed and ached while I finger fucked the Fae man. I slid my fingers in and out, harder and faster while he writhed and moaned with pleasure.

"My turn," Zared said. He waited until I slid my fingers out before tentatively replacing them with his own, larger fingers. His throat bobbed as he swallowed, but in a matter of moments he thrusted as firm as I had.

"Gods yes," Tavian groaned.

He rolled onto his side until I was able to slip my lips over his cock. With both of us working him from either side, he was powerless to do anything but cum with a series of breathy groans and grunts, spilling his cum into my mouth.

"Swallow it," Zared said insistently.

I lifted my head up high enough for both of them to see, then deliberately swallowed down every delicious drop.

"Good girl. Come here," Zared ordered. He pushed Tavian gently back onto his stomach and grabbed my hand until I was sitting on Tavian's back, my legs to either side of me to take most of my weight.

Zared ran his hand up and down his cock a couple of times, then positioned it just outside Tavian's ass. His eyes half closed in concentration, he pressed himself inside. At the same time, he slid his hand down to rub over my clit and kissed my mouth.

I leaned back a little and wrapped my legs around Zared's waist.

Feeling him sliding in and out of Tavian while working me was one of the hottest things I'd ever experienced.

Judging by the moans and groans from Tavian, he felt the same way.

"Fuck, this is..." Zared ground out between kisses. "So fucking good." He thrust into Tavian with smooth, even strokes, matching those with circles around my clit. "Come for me."

I didn't want to come so quickly, but I couldn't contain it. Everything about this was so erotic. I tipped over the edge, groaning and dripping all over Zared's fingers and Tavian's back.

Zared came a moment or two later, his body still with heavy tension until his balls released his hot cum into Tavian's ass. He bit down on my lip at the same time, forcing a second orgasm out of me from sheer delight at the pain. Not even the coppery taste of my blood could deter me from the burst of pleasure.

Zared panted against my mouth for a long while before sliding his cock free.

"Any time you want to do this again, I'm all for it," Tavian said. "Although, my cock is already hard again." He made a face of mild discomfort.

"Good," Zared said. "Fuck her." He placed his hands on my hips and raised me up so Tavian could roll over onto his back. Carefully, he lowered me onto Tavian's erect cock.

"Yes, sir," Tavian said breathlessly. He placed his

hands on my waist, just above Zared's and thrust up into me as I looked Zared in the eyes.

Zared worked his hand back between us and over my clit again. "I want you both to come at the same time."

I didn't think I had another orgasm in me until I heard those words. The moment they were out of his mouth, another burst of desire rose inside me. The need to please him as well as the need to feel good. It wasn't the same as the need to please an alpha. This was the desire to please my lover, to let him dominate Tavian and me. In this moment, he could have asked almost anything and we would have done it. An orgasm seemed like a small thing to give him.

When it came, it was a big thing, intense, travelling all the way through my body, clenching Tavian's cock and drawing a second orgasm out of him at the same time.

My breasts bounced as I ground onto Zared's hand and Tavian's cock. All thought went out of my head except the extreme pleasure as I shattered completely, coming apart around them in a flood of my cum and Tavian's.

I cried out long and loud until I came back down to earth with a sag and breathless pants. Tavian sounded much the same way, puffing and sagging back against the mattress.

"Gods, you two are amazing," Tavian whispered.

"I was going to say the same about you two," I said.

"I'm glad you came for me," Zared said. "In both meanings of the word."

"We'll always come for you," Tavian told him. "Always."

An exhausted murmur of agreement was all I could manage. I was definitely eager to do this again.

26

KHALA

"Do you come here often?" I asked. We stepped through the portal and onto the paved street that led to the Autumn Court's palace.

Cavan raised his elegant eyebrows at me but didn't answer.

Marial was undeniably magnificent. Tall towers swept toward the sky, each looking as though they were made from red-brown leaves.

Elegant bridges stretched across a river that glimmered like polished copper in the early morning light. The iron railing on either side was formed into the shapes of leaves, the top rail worn smooth from countless years of hands swiping past.

The streets were lined with shops, all in neat rows.

Their storefronts were each adorned with autumnal colours of orange, red, and gold.

Even this early, the conversations of merchants and patrons filled the streets. Each one seeming tense, forced.

The buildings closer to the palace were all constructed of dark stone and iron, also giving the appearance they were made of leaves.

I stopped to appreciate the way they were cut and placed with such careful precision. Masons must have taken years to perfect the art. Constructing each one would have taken the better part of a year. The effect was striking.

I felt as if I was encased in autumn.

"Through here." Cavan led me toward a set of tall gates with the same pattern as the bridge railing. "Remember you're obedient, broken and very sorry you were rude to him."

"I'm not sure I can fake the last one," I muttered.

"Try, or I'll order you," he said simply.

"Have I mentioned how unfair that is?" I glanced sideways at him.

"You might have mentioned it. In this instance, it might work in our favour. Perhaps I should order you now and save any potential hassle later." He gave me a speculative look in return.

"I think you just want me on my knees." I kept my eyes down, as though I really was beaten.

"I definitely want you on your knees," he replied. "But not if I have to order you. Where's the fun in that?"

"You're not shy about asking for what you want," I observed.

He chuckled. "I've always found it easier to be forthcoming. So to speak."

"Even if Ryze wants to stab you every time you look at me?"

"Especially then," he agreed. "I've never let someone like him get in my way. I don't intend to start now."

I was attracted to him, in spite of the complications. Maybe in part because of it. Nothing worth having was never easy.

For now though, I needed to concentrate on why we were here.

I deliberately flinched away from the guards as we walked through the gate, and wrapped my arms around myself. I felt the weight of their gazes on me, but none made a move to stop us. As far as they knew, we were what we appeared to be. The High Lord of the Summer Court and his broken omega.

The palace itself was a sprawling building made of a lighter stone than the rest of the city. If Marial was the red of autumn, the palace was the yellow and gold. Towers, spires, and domes topped the vast complex, each one covered in what looked like shining gold leaf, adorned with intricate carvings of autumn leaves and vines.

"Walk a little behind me," Cavan muttered before we stepped through the enormous doors that led into a wide courtyard. "But stay close. Act like I own you now and you know it."

"You're having way too much fun with this," I whispered back.

"Yes, and I intend to keep having fun with it. Quiet now. Let me do the talking."

I swallowed hard. Gods, that was hotter than it should be.

I followed him through the courtyard, my eyes on his way too perfect ass.

I was enveloped in the rich, spicy scent of autumn.

The air was cool and crisp. The leaves on the trees rustled gently in the breeze. Here, it felt like the unseasonable warmth everywhere else didn't exist.

I sensed it was exactly like this regardless of the time of year, or the season. Undoubtedly the result of some kind of magic.

We were greeted by more guards in front of a door that led into the palace. They looked like they might stop us from entering until they realised who Cavan was.

"High Lord Cavan." One snapped to attention. His eyes slid to me for a moment, then away like I was nothing more than a dog at Cavan's heels.

I forced my eyes down lower before my annoyance was too obvious. We'd never find the key if we didn't even make it through the door.

"You can announce my arrival to High Lord Harel," Cavan instructed.

"Yes, my Lord." The guards jumped to do as he was told. He hurried inside and spoke to someone.

After what felt like ages, he re-emerged. "My Lord will see you." He stepped aside to let us in.

"Of course he will." Cavan swept past like he owned the place. He was the absolute epitome of arrogance. If I had to decide who was cockier, him or Ryze, I'd be hard pressed to do it.

I hurried along behind him, keeping as much distance from the guards as I could.

I even managed to ignore when one of them muttered something about me being, "The Lord of Summer's slut." Apparently the Autumn Court Fae were all judgemental assholes.

The inside of the palace was as stunning as the outside. The walls were covered with tapestries of golden leaves, and richly coloured murals depicting the different seasons.

The floors were made of polished red-brown stone

which reflected the sunlight that slanted through wide windows set high in the wall. Chandeliers dangled from the ceiling, dripping with gold and glass. Like everywhere else, they were shaped like leaves.

We were greeted by a courtier dressed in autumnal colours, and a couple of other guards.

"Lord Cavan," the courtier said smoothly. "To what do we owe the pleasure of your presence today?"

"Daniek." Cavan sounded bored. "I've come to meet with Harel. I'm sure you wouldn't want to keep him waiting."

Daniek smiled ingratiatingly. "Of course not. Come along then." He barely managed to contain his irritation at Cavan's obvious disinterest in telling him anything.

Hopefully I was better at containing my smirk. People like Daniek liked to gather up gossip, and didn't mind spreading it around. I'd bet the moment he was away from us, he'd be telling someone about us, and speculating about the reason for our visit.

Once again, I hurried along behind Cavan as if I was scared to let him out of my sight. I kept my gaze at the floor, trying to cover my annoyance.

I'd never been shy, or timid. Pretending to be so now was difficult and uncomfortable.

Better than being ordered to behave this way. If

nothing else, the situation reminded me how vulnerable omegas were to alphas.

The throne room was perhaps the most magnificent thing I'd seen since stepping foot in Marial.

The walls were lined with mirrors that reflected light from two ornate chandeliers, making the room glow with warm, golden light.

The throne itself was carved from dark mahogany, and inlaid with rubies and topaz, and yet more gold leaf in the shape of leaves. No one would ever mistake which court we were in.

I glanced up briefly to see Harel on the throne, legs crossed at his knees. He looked at Cavan like he was a supplicant come to beg for his favour.

He looked at me like I was less than nothing.

I forced my eyes back down before I told him to fuck off again.

"Isn't this an interesting surprise," Harel drawled. "Cavan, and Ryze's whore. Or is she yours now? Perhaps she spreads her legs for both of you?"

I ducked my head down lower, as though ashamed of his words instead of being pissed off as fuck.

"Ryze got tired of her attitude," Cavan said. "He gave her to me to teach her how to behave. She didn't learn quickly, but she learnt thoroughly. I thought you'd appreciate seeing her, since she put our alliance in jeopardy. She's been a lot of trouble, but she's very sorry for every, every moment of it."

He gave the impression he beat me until my skin was raw and I was begging him to stop. Which led me to wonder what it would feel like if he spanked me.

Focus, I told myself.

"Is she now?" Harel slid off his throne and stepped towards us. He grabbed my chin in a tight grip and forced my face up.

I averted my eyes and swallowed like I was scared instead of in pain from the way his fingers dug into me.

"This is a delightful change from the mouthy slut. If I'm convinced she really is as broken as you say she is."

"Why would I bother to lie about something like that?" Cavan asked, sounding bored again.

"Perhaps your new allies proved unreliable," Harel said. "You wanted a way back into my good graces."

Only by sheer will, I managed to contain a snort. He wasn't just an asshole, he was delusional.

"I was never going to align with Ryzellius or Thiron," Cavan said. "They believed my reasoning for bringing all those omegas to my court. As a gesture of good faith, Ryze left this one with me. She's used goods, but when she's on her knees, she can do incredible things with her mouth."

"They actually think those other courts are real?" Harel asked derisively.

"I don't care what they think," Cavan said. "They'll stay out of my way the next time the Temple moves any potential omegas. Out of *our* way."

"So you're keeping your promise to send some to me." Harel leaned in until his breath brushed my cheek.

I didn't need to fake my trembling. Being this close to him made me want to jerk my face away and drive my knee into his groin. I smelled alpha on him, thick and unyielding.

Cavan better fucking know what he was doing.

"Of course," Cavan said lightly. "We have an agreement. We build our magic and our courts become more powerful. When the time comes, we move against The Spring and Winter Courts."

That was exactly what Ryze assumed Cavan and Harel were up to in the first place. It sounded chilling coming from his mouth. Hopefully it wasn't the truth after all. If it was, he'd get a whole lot more than a knee in his groin.

Harel shoved me away so hard I almost fell on my ass.

I managed to keep my footing and moved closer to Cavan, as though scared of Harel. Honestly, I was ready to see if I could freeze or boil his brain. Maybe one, then the other.

Harel chuckled. "I like her much better like this. I'd

insist on borrowing her, but I don't like 'used goods,' as you put it. Especially if Ryze had his cock in her. Broken or not, she's still a tainted whore. What will you do when you tire of her?"

"I'll give her to my men to play with," Cavan replied. "They aren't so fussy about where their pussy comes from."

As disgusting as this conversation was, I was relieved Harel had no interest in touching me. For a moment there, I thought he might insist on being shown I was broken.

The last thing I wanted was any of his body parts inside any of mine.

I shuddered.

Let them think it was because I was fearful of a future in which I was passed around Cavan's guards. That wasn't a lie, I didn't want that to happen either.

27

———

KHALA

"It seems we have a lot to discuss." Harel flopped back onto his throne so heavily I was surprised it didn't break. Judging by the wear on the seat and the arms, it was as old as either of the Fae men. It must be well made to withstand that kind of treatment.

"Indeed we do," Cavan agreed. "I appreciate the opportunity to enjoy your hospitality."

"I'm sure you do." Harel hadn't offered, but Cavan worded it in a way that he'd be rude to decline.

I didn't think Harel gave a fuck about being rude, but presumably there was some protocol between High Lords, especially when there were courtiers hovering nearby.

Harel waved one of them over and told them to tell the kitchen to prepare for a lunch guest. Evidently I didn't exist. That was fine with me. The sooner he forgot about me, the better.

"Make a room too," Harel added. "I'm sure Cavan will want to stay for a night or two." He looked like he wanted Cavan to refuse, but Cavan smiled.

"It would be my pleasure. Only for a night or two. I wouldn't want to impose any longer than that."

"Of course." That was obviously too much by Harel's standards, but if nothing else, he needed the alliance. Wanted the omegas and their magic.

What did Ryze say about Autumn Court magic? That it was related to death. That didn't sound like a power Jorius needed more of.

"If you'll follow me, I'll show you to your room," Daniek said. "I'm sure you'd like to rest before lunch."

"Certainly," Cavan agreed.

Considering the day's exercise consisted of making a portal from Havenmoor, stepping through it, and walking through the streets of Marial for ten or twenty minutes, I didn't think a rest was warranted.

On the other hand, I was happy to be away from Harel and his courtiers. I hadn't looked, but I knew they were watching, listening and judging. I didn't care what they thought, but I didn't want to be on display either.

I stayed close to Cavan as we followed Daniek out of the throne room and down the ornate corridor.

Like everywhere else in the Autumn Court, the bedroom the courtier led us to was opulent.

The air was thick with the scent of sandalwood. The walls were adorned with tapestries depicting scenes of what I assumed were Fae mythology. Rich autumn colors adorned every surface, from the yellow-gold curtains to the russet velvet cushions piled high on the enormous four-poster bed.

The bed was made of carved oak, with intricately detailed posts which reached almost to the high ceiling. Silk sheets embroidered with gold thread were tucked in neatly across the top of the mattress and pillows.

Matching nightstands sat on either side of the bed, their carved wooden legs gleaming. A plush armchair stood in each corner, their front feet sinking into thick woven rugs on the polished wooden floor.

Sunlight poured through a set of double doors that led out to a balcony overlooking lush gardens below.

At the far end of the room, a fireplace dominated the wall, its stone mantel intricately, and somewhat excessively, covered with carvings of flowers and animals. It looked as though a fire hadn't been lit in there for a long time.

"Thank you." Cavan dismissed Daniek with a nod.

The courtier looked less than pleased, but he

backed out the door and closed it behind him with a bow.

Cavan sighed and his posture relaxed visibly.

"He doesn't spare any expense, does he?" I looked around at everything. It must have cost a High Lord's ransom just to decorate this room.

"Not when he's trying to impress his guest," Cavan agreed.

"Guest, singular." I raised an eyebrow at him. "He doesn't like to make a girl feel welcome, does he?"

"Harel isn't a fan of women," he said.

"You don't say," I said sarcastically. "He doesn't seem to be a fan of anyone but himself. You didn't mean any of that, did you?"

I placed my hands on my hips and gave him a level look. The ability to look him almost eye to eye might be one of my favourite things about being Fae. If I was human, I'd have to crane my neck.

"Which bit?" he asked, feigning innocence.

"Most of it," I told him. "You're not really gathering omegas for our power, right? You're not planning to invade the other courts? You're certainly not handing me over to your men."

"No. No. And definitely *not*," he said. "I bet I wasn't lying about your mouth."

He stepped towards me, gripped my shoulders and

pushed me until my back was against one of the bed posts.

Heart racing, I looked back at him. "Did you and my mother ever..." I wasn't sure why I needed the answer to that, but I did.

His responding smile was brief, but he clearly understood why I asked the question.

"No, never. Her heart and body were always with your father."

Relief rushed through me. I wasn't sure what I'd do if his answer was yes, but I was fucking glad it wasn't.

"And mine are with you," he added before he slammed his lips down onto mine.

I'd thought about doing this a lot, in spite of my connection with the other four men. He didn't disappoint.

I slipped my arms around his neck and kissed him back.

"How's that?" I asked when I finally broke off the kiss.

"Good for a start." He scooped me up like I weighed nothing and placed me on the bed.

While my heart raced, he started to slowly undress me, bit by bit, kissing my skin as he bared it.

"I've been thinking," he said as he traced lines across my stomach with his tongue. "If you're supposed to be broken, shouldn't you know how it feels to be spanked?"

"How do you know I don't already know?" I replied.

He picked up his head and cocked it at me. "Do you?"

"Yes," I admitted. "I wasn't always perfectly behaved when I was a Silent Maiden."

He chuckled. "Why does that not surprise me in the least?"

"I have no idea, I'm sure," I said innocently. "Maybe they strapped me for their own enjoyment."

His mouth drew back. "That wouldn't surprise me either. What about you, though? Did you enjoy it?"

"Is it wrong if I say I did?" I winced.

"Not even a little bit," he assured me. "Would you like to feel it again?" He kissed around my belly button.

Fuck yes, please.

"Do I have a choice?" I asked teasingly. "If you own me, shouldn't you do whatever you want with me?"

He turned his face to the side so his cheek was resting on my belly. "Good point. I think I will. But tell me if I go too far for you."

"If you go too far, you'll know about it," I assured him.

"Just make sure to be loud," he said. "No doubt someone will be listening. You might as well make it sound convincing."

"It sounds like we need a safe word then," I said. "If I'm supposed to be screaming at you to stop, then I might send you the wrong message."

"Good point," he said. "Let's go with something in context, but that you might not shout out in pleasure. Something like, *I hate you.*"

I grinned. "It's good to see you're as crazy as all the other Fae. If you're supposed to be sadistic, that isn't going to stop you."

He blew a warm breath across my stomach. "You're right. Maybe something like 'yellow.' If anyone was listening at the door, it would sound like, hells no."

"Suitably sadistic, but just about right." I nodded.

"Good. Now be a good slut and roll over onto your stomach."

I gave him a look but did what he said.

"I've been waiting for this for too long." He nibbled at my ass cheek until I wriggled. Chuckling, he propped himself up on his elbow and brought his hand down hard on my bare skin.

A shock of pain and pleasure surged through me, sending heat to my core. I groaned in pleasure.

"You like that?" He brought his hand down again, harder this time.

I gasped out my nose. My whole body was trembling with need. I wanted him to keep spanking me. At the same time, I wanted him to drive himself deep inside me. To pound into me until I screamed.

"Harder," I said breathlessly.

"Is that how an omega talks when she addresses the alpha who owns her?" he asked.

I whimpered. "Harder, please, alpha."

"That's better." He slapped me harder and harder, until my eyes started to water.

My pussy was dripping by now. My senses were in overdrive. I sucked in a breath. The dominant alpha scent of him filled my nostrils and flooded through me, right down to the heat between my thighs.

I cried out louder with each strike, part pleasure, part pain. Right before I shouted out yellow and begged him to stop, he stopped.

I wasn't aware of him removing his pants, but then he was parting my legs with his hands and sliding his cock inside me.

He leaned over and spoke into my ear. "Your ass is a perfect shade of red."

"Perfect for the Autumn Court, alpha?" I asked jokingly.

"Perfect for anywhere, omega," he replied. He began a series of slow, lazy thrusts into me. "You're perfect for anywhere."

His cock felt so incredible, driving into me, pure pleasure after all the pain.

He slipped out of me, rolled me over into my back and knelt between my legs. He slid his hands under my thighs and cupped my ass. He pulled me forward until only my shoulders and head rested on the mattress, my back suspended in the air between us.

I wrapped my legs around his hips as he pressed his cock back into me.

I placed my arms to either side of me, bracing me and using my hands to rock my hips in rhythm with his thrusts.

I locked my eyes on his and watched his expression of bliss as he pounded over and over again into my body.

"Gods, you feel incredible," he whispered.

"So do you," I said back. With every thrust, his knot rubbed and nudged my clit, driving me ever closer to an orgasm.

"You don't hate me?" he teased.

"I definitely do," I joked. "Such an asshole, alpha." I rocked harder, drawing closer and closer.

"It seems I didn't spank you hard enough." He grinned.

"Oh you did," I assured him. I scrunched my eyes closed.

"Keep them open," he said. "I want your eyes on me when you come. Look right at my face."

I opened them and focused on his intense blue

eyes. The colour of the sky in the middle of summer. He was the epitome of his court. Bright and hot and compelling. The more I got of him, the more I wanted. The more I needed.

I arched my back as I came around his cock. The smile that graced his lips brought me higher and higher, before breaking me apart in the most perfect, explosive way possible.

My pussy milked his cock, pulling an orgasm out of him. His whole body went rigid and still. He grunted hard, grinding himself against me, spilling himself inside me.

"Fucking gods, yes," he breathed. "Khala you are... everything." He sagged forward, panting heavily before lowering us both down to the mattress and pulling me close to him.

For a long time we lay there in silence, enjoying each other's company and letting the sweat on our bodies dry.

28

KHALA

My breath held, I moved through the shadows of the palace halls.

Cavan was dining with Harel and his favourite courtiers, keeping them distracted for as long as he could.

Apparently I was confined to his room as punishment for something. Presumably they bought that story, because when I slipped out an hour later, there were no guards at the door. If anything bad happened to me, it would be my fault.

So hospitable.

On bare feet, I stepped silently. The only sound was the occasional swish of fabric on fabric, and laughter from somewhere else in the palace.

Harel's booming voice echoed, followed by more

laughter. The polite kind, as though the listeners were humouring him, not enjoying his humour.

I hurried on as quickly as I could, the map Cavan drew etched in my mind.

"I'm not certain the key is here, but it is a possibility," he'd said, his fingertip pressed to the shape of one room. "I don't know this place as well as I probably should."

"I'm guessing you know it better than Ryze, or even Tavian," I said. "I'll look there, but what if I don't find it?"

"Then keep looking. Otherwise, I'm going to have to do something drastic." He ran a hand over my slightly sore ass.

"Spanking me again won't make the key magically appear," I pointed out.

"No, but we'd both enjoy it." He pinched my ass and grinned when I jumped.

I batted his hand away. "I'm also not going to try to seduce Harel to find out where the key is. Even if he was interested in used goods." I grimaced.

"Then you better find the key," he said.

"You better be right about it being where you think it is," I retorted.

The dimly lit walls were covered in intricate tapestries showing scenes of hunting and feasting. Their appearance seemed distorted somehow, like they were stretched too thin or at too much of an angle. Perhaps the loom wasn't set straight.

Hells, for all I knew, it was a preferred style here in this court.

I froze as voices came up a corridor that crossed the one I was in. I ducked back and tucked myself into an alcove as a group of courtiers passed by.

They laughed and chatted, their voices echoing down the hall. I only half-listened to what they were saying. Something about the weather and an upcoming wedding. None seemed particularly interested. If anything, I got the impression they were mocking the couple preparing to exchange vows.

As soon as they were out of sight, I pressed on, keeping to the shadows. The palace seemed endless, with hallways branching off in every direction. Every so often, I stopped to picture the map in my mind. I would have carried it with me, but as Cavan pointed out, I had no reason to be sneaking around the palace with a map in my hand.

Or without a map in my hand, but I could make up an excuse if anyone saw me.

Finally, I reached a small room tucked away at the end of a long hallway.

It wasn't opulent like the rest of the palace. That in itself was peculiar. On the other hand, where better to keep a hidden key than in a room that seemed ordinary and uninteresting?

Although, now I thought about it, that was as suspicious as fuck. Since pretty much everything I'd seen since we stepped foot in Marial fit into that category, I slipped into the room and closed the door behind me.

I illuminated the room with magic and started to hunt around.

"What the hells?"

I moved closer, my breath catching in my throat as I stared. In the center of the room was a throne made of twisted branches and thorns. It reminded me of the song on the maps. Twisted branches that had the answers, or something like that.

Did Cavan know this was here?

I stepped around it, eyes on it as though it might jump out at me or something.

"It's just a chair," I told myself.

My whisper almost made me jump. It sounded too loud in the silence. This whole sneaking around thing had me on edge, it was totally not the weird throne.

All right, it was equal parts of both. I'd seen some odd things in the last couple of months, this was just the most recent.

I tentatively put my hand out to touch it, careful not to prick myself on a thorn.

I remembered a tale I was told as a young Silent Maiden, of a goddess who did exactly that. She bled so much from that tiny pinprick, she passed out.

When she woke up, a thousand years had passed. Her children had all grown up. Her husband gave up on her ever returning from wherever she supposedly went, and married some other goddess.

Heartbroken, she killed her husband and his new wife before disappearing into the sky to become a shooting star.

Since all of that would suck, I was careful to avoid anything pointy and sharp.

The branches were still ragged, the wood rough under my fingertip. It felt like someone picked a bunch of sticks up off the ground and formed them into a throne. And yet, where my skin touched, I felt a faint tingle, like there was magic embedded in the chair.

"It doesn't usually let anyone touch it," a voice said from behind me.

I jumped back from the throne and whirled around. I hadn't even heard the door open, but now Illaria stood in the doorway, a candle in her hand.

"You scared the shit out of me," I told her. "What are you doing here?"

I couldn't immediately tell if she was armed or not, but after she distracted Tavian back in Garial, I could only assume her agenda was suspicious as fuck.

Fitting for the Autumn Court.

"I could ask you the same thing, but I already know," she said. "You're looking for the key."

"I don't know what you're talking about," I said, shrugging one shoulder.

"Why else would you be in my father's court, unless you are searching for some way to find the missing courts?"

"Your father's court?" I echoed. "Harel is your father?"

She sighed and stepped further into the room before closing the door behind her.

"Unfortunately, yes. I've been in exile in the Winter Court for a long while. I thought it was time to come back and beg for my father's forgiveness." She grimaced.

"You're looking for the key?" I guessed.

"I know where the key is," she said. "I'm here to help you find it. I went back to the Winter Court, only to hear you'd gone to Havenmoor. I could have saved you that time. Would have if it wasn't for the first attack. I was supposed to distract Tavian, so my contacts could speak to High Lord Ryzellius. They suspected the attack might come. They wanted Tavian away from it, so he wouldn't be harmed."

I shook my head. "I don't understand. Who are your contacts?"

"Other people in the Autumn Court who believe in the other courts," she replied. "We believe the Court of Dreams will be the salvation of the seasonal courts."

She sounded dogmatic, and slightly unhinged.

"Salvation from what?" I asked.

"From division, apathy and antagonism," she said. "You know of how High Lord Cavan has tried to unite the seasonal courts. He's been ignored and ridiculed. Vilified. We believe Fae from the Court of Shadows have been working for a long time to create exactly that environment. When they awaken the rest of the court, that will be to their advantage. If the seasonal courts are pitted against each other, they can use that weakness. Even if it means stepping over bones and ashes."

Her words reminded me of what Tavian said of his vision.

"They want us to go to war against each other, so they can step in at the end and defeat all of us?" I said slowly.

"Exactly." She nodded. The movement made her candle flicker.

"And you think the Court of Dreams can help stop that from happening?"

"They already are. Every time the Court of Shadows opens a portal, they piggyback their magic on to whatever is being sent through. There are Fae in the seasonal courts with the blood of the Court of Dreams. And the Court of Shadows," she added.

"When the portal opens, they can use that magic," I said.

"I think you know people who can," she said. "Who are."

I certainly did. Tavian's visions, for one. If he had the blood of the lost courts inside him, he might be a seer. Hycanthe, whose magic increased in strength whenever a portal opened, for another.

"Shouldn't that blood be diluted by now?"

Illaria laughed softly. "Fae can bear children at hundreds of years old. Those with the blood of those courts may be children of the lost Fae. Grandchildren at most."

"Is it possible those attacks are aimed at someone in particular?" I asked carefully.

"Not only possible, it's likely," she said. "The lost courts can only be returned by a coming together of a Fae with the blood of the Court of Shadows, one with the blood of the Court of Dreams, and one whose blood transcends courts. There are some who believe it's possible to return one court and not the other. Both of those courts are trying to stop the other from being awakened. As far as we can determine, the Court of Dreams has only been defending itself."

"You sound like you know a lot about all of this," I said.

"The people I work with have been looking into this since before Cavan," she said. "We've been working in the shadows, trying to help him be heard. That's why I got exiled. My father doesn't believe any of it. A lot of people don't. Some of us wanted to approach Cavan directly, but we didn't dare reveal ourselves. If my father knew I was talking to you right now, I'd be executed in the morning. In public, as a warning to the others."

"Sounds like a loving parent," I said sarcastically.

"There's nothing my father won't do to get his way," she said. "To save face. Having a daughter who openly disagreed with him caused him humiliation. It would have been bad enough if I stood outside and told him the sky was pink. When it comes to the other courts, he has no room for leniency. Or forgiveness, which is why I'm leaving before the sun rises. I needed you to find what you came here to find. I would have taken it, but he would have known. He has eyes on me; he thinks I haven't noticed. I don't know how long it'll be before they realise I'm out of their sight."

"You should talk to Cavan," I said. "It sounds like you have the answers to a lot of his questions."

"I only know what I've told you," she said. "And that my people suspect Tavian has Court of Dreams blood

on his father's side. The High Lord had a brief relation-
ship with a priestess. Thirteen months later, he was
born. That's the gestation period for Fae."

I winced. Nine months sounded like long enough
to me.

"And you have suspicions about Hycanthe too," I
said.

"I wasn't sure if it was her, you or Jezalyn," Illaria
said. "We figured it was one of you, because things
escalated after the removal of your chokers. They were
dampening more than the mating urge, or your ability
to speak."

"One of us has lost court blood?" I presumed it
wasn't me, unless my mother carried the blood and
Cavan didn't know.

"Wait, Tavian's father might be a High Lord? Does
that make him the heir?"

"We can only guess at that," she replied. "We don't
know who amongst those Fae still live. For all we know,
one of you former maidens might be the heir to the
Court of Shadows."

"My money is on Hycanthe," I said dryly. If they
were as nasty as they sounded, that fit. Her money
would probably be on me, so I supposed that made us
even.

"You might be right, you might not. Either way, you
need to find the key and, from what I gather from the

map in Havenmoor, that will lead you to the place that has the answers. What might happen there, I have no idea."

"How do you know about the keys?" I asked.

She smiled humourlessly. "I'm my father's heir. He'd dearly like a better one. Preferably a male who does what he says. In the meantime, I had to know where it is, in case something happened to him."

"Where is it?" I asked.

She explained where, and how to get it.

"The trick will be getting in and out without being seen."

"Right." Of course it couldn't be easy. Nothing about this had been yet, why would it start now?

"This is the real throne of the Autumn Court." She brushed the tips of her fingers over the back of it, apparently not worried about being pricked. "My father replaced it when he became High Lord. He said it was too uncomfortable."

"It doesn't look very comfortable," I said.

"It's not supposed to be. It's a symbol of our court."

"Is that your way of saying it's a chair, but no one is supposed to sit on it?" I asked.

She laughed softly. "Something like that. You have to want to be High Lord very much to sit in a chair like that."

"Or you have to have to be willing to change out the chair," I said.

"That too," she agreed.

"Are you sure you can't get the key for me?" I asked. Presumably she could go places in the palace without being asked questions, unlike me.

"I've lingered for too long already," she said. "I need to return to my father's banquet. I'll stay to say my good nights. As soon as I slip away, he'll check to see if the key is still there. Once he's left, you can make your move."

"How can I be sure this isn't a trap?" I asked. "You might be working for this faction you talk about, or you might be working for your father. He may be waiting for me if I sneak in there."

"He might be," she agreed. "But if he is, it's nothing to do with me. I can promise you that."

I wasn't sure if I could believe her promises, but she was forthcoming with a lot of answers to a lot of questions. Assuming it wasn't all a bunch of lies.

"You can keep searching for the key, or you can look for it when I said it was. When you find it there, then you might believe me. Since you won't find it anywhere else, it's worth a try. Right?"

"Those sound like famous last words if I ever heard them," I remarked.

"I need to go. I'm sure we'll be seeing each other

again. Especially if that handsome human is with you." She flashed a smile.

A totally irrational surge of annoyance passed through me. I knew she didn't mean anything by it, but Zared was mine. A part of my pack.

She gave me a knowing look, then slipped out the door.

I waited a minute or two, then followed her. I didn't know which direction she'd gone, but there was no sign of her now. Or anyone else in the corridor outside. Judging by the talking and laughter, the banquet was still in full swing.

I slipped back into the room I shared with Cavan without seeing anyone else.

29

——————

KHALA

"That complicates things," Cavan said.

"Just a little," I agreed. "I'm sure you have a plan."

"While I appreciate your faith in me," he said slowly, "you'll have to give me a moment."

I couldn't resist teasing him. "I knew I should have brought Ryze. He seems to know all about sneaking around. He'd be in and out of there by now."

"Do you want me to spank you again?" he growled.

"Maybe I do," I replied tartly. "Or maybe we can figure out a way to get this fucking key and get out of here."

"First that, then the other." He placed his hands to either side of him on the bed and pushed himself to his feet. "Come on then."

"You have a plan?" I rose to follow him.

"No, I figured we'd work it out as we went along. Harel and everyone else turned in hours ago. Judging by the amount of wine they drank, they won't be up early, so we have some time. We need to keep an eye out for guards. Whatever I say, play along."

"Why do I think that sounds like the start of a very bad idea?" I asked.

He smiled before he opened the door and stepped out, leaving me to scurry along behind him.

Like he did everywhere else, he strode along like he owned the place. Between him and Ryze, they had at least three quarters of the confidence that existed in the seasonal courts.

We approached a couple of guards who were patrolling the corridor. Against what, I didn't know. People like us, I supposed.

"Hurry up," Cavan snapped over his shoulder. "Unless you enjoyed your punishment for being too slow the last time. I can give you double."

I didn't hate the sound of that, but I kept my eyes down and trotted until I caught up. "Sorry," I muttered.

He stopped so quickly I almost ran into the back of him.

"Sorry what?" he growled.

"Sorry, alpha," I said quickly. Asshole was enjoying this way too much. If he wasn't careful, I'd bite his cock. Not in a good way.

He glared at me, then turned and stomped on.

The guards looked at me and one of them actually chuckled. He was an asshole too.

I followed Cavan around the corner, before punching him in the arm.

"Ouch what was that for?" He rubbed the spot which probably didn't hurt, because I didn't punch him *that* hard.

"I felt like it," I said. "Are you suggesting you didn't deserve it?"

He grinned. "Stay in your role. You never know when someone else might appear."

"Yes, sir," I said sarcastically. I sighed and slumped back down beside him.

"I like the way that sounds," he said.

"Of course you do," I whispered.

He gestured for me to be quiet as we walked down another corridor and into the one leading to the throne room.

"You'd think he'd keep it somewhere safer, like a treasury," I remarked. "Or under his pillow. No one would want to go there to find it."

"Lucky for you it's not under there," Cavan said. "Otherwise I'd have to send you for it. Whatever happened there, you'd have to play along."

"I'm starting to think the sadistic thing isn't an act," I told him. I was almost certain he didn't mean he'd let

Harel do whatever he wanted to me. I sure as hells wouldn't.

"Quiet." He tried the door to the throne room. It was locked. A quick flick of his finger and flare of magic, and it clicked open.

"Locks are only there to keep out honest people and people who can't do magic," he said.

"I know which of those you fit into," I said sweetly.

He snorted.

We stepped inside and he closed the door behind us.

The darkness inside was almost suffocating. The only light came from the moon. It cast an eerie glow through the window, illuminating the room in patches. It was quiet, too quiet. the stillness broken only by the sound of our footsteps on the cold, hard floor.

"I don't know about this," I said. "It feels..."

"Like we shouldn't be here?" he asked.

"Exactly," I agreed. "Entering places like this was something Zared and I used to do when I was a maiden."

"Why is that a problem now?" He cocked his head as he illuminated the room with magic on his hand.

"I don't know. I suppose I think Fae should behave differently. More mature or something. Aren't we supposed to be regal and elegant?"

"Of course, but that doesn't mean we have to be

boring." He waved his hand across the arm of the chair and looked down and around. "Nothing on this side."

I looked around the other. "I can't see— Wait." I slid my hand across a groove in the wood. It was round and smooth. "If I stick my finger in this, am I going to end up dead?"

"Potentially," he said. "Do you want me to do it? I can if you're scared." He gave me a challenging look I was almost certain he knew I'd have to refuse.

Asshole.

"I'm not scared," I said. "All right, I am, but if I end up dead, I'm going to be really, really pissed off at you."

"Save your pissed off for Harel," he said. "If there's a booby trap in there, it's because he put it there."

"That would be no consolation if I was dead." I placed my finger into the groove and pressed down into it. I heard a soft click and a drawer slid out from under the arm of the throne.

Inside was what looked like a rusty, old key.

"Please tell me that's what we're looking for," I said.

"You were expecting something shiny?" he asked.

"Well...yes." My fingers hovered over the key. "I think this is the first rusty thing I've seen since I left Ebonfalls."

"Ryze and I are about as rusty as that," he said with a smile. "Pick it up."

I tentatively touched the key, then gripped it

between my thumb and forefinger. When I lifted it up out of the drawer, it glinted in the moonlight.

"What the fuck?" It didn't look rusty anymore. It was as shiny as one of Tavian's knives.

"A little autumn magic. Making it look like nothing when it's really something. Here." He reached into his pocket. "You didn't think I'd come unprepared did you?"

He held a similar-looking key on the palm of his hand.

"If Harel has a quick look, he'll assume the key is still there." He handed it to me and pocketed the other one.

I placed the replacement in the drawer and shook my head as it turned rusty.

"Can I learn to do that?"

"You could if you had your first heat with Harel or an alpha here. I'll let you decide if it's worth it or not."

"That would be a big no," I said. "We should get out of here."

"We could," he said slowly. "Or we could stay here a little longer." He reached over and closed the drawer, then grabbed my wrist and pulled me until I was sitting on Harel's throne.

"You like living dangerously," I observed.

"If those guards talk about seeing us in the corridor, we can say I brought you here for this. It's the kind of depraved thing Harel would expect of any of the other High Lords."

He hooked his fingers into the top of my pants and tugged them down my hips. He pulled them until he was able to slide one leg off my foot.

"Would you want any of them to do this on your throne?" I asked as he pressed my thighs apart with his hands and knelt in front of me.

"If anyone other than me fucks on my throne, I'll have them executed." He lowered his mouth and ran his tongue all the way from the bottom of my pussy to the top.

I shivered. There was something both enticing and arousing about him fucking me in a place like this. I should have told him to stop, but I didn't want to. Instead, I leaned back against the mahogany and enjoyed the way he devoured me.

"You taste like divine sin," he said. "Absolutely delicious."

I groaned and rocked against his mouth, slowly, building the friction. He certainly knew what to do with his tongue. And his fingers, three of which he slid deep inside me.

In the moonlight, in the throne room, the High Lord of the Summer Court fucked me with his hand and tongue. He drove me to the edge and drew back to let me come down before driving me harder still.

Several times, he pushed me right to the brink, only to pull back before I tipped over.

After the fourth time, I growled at him.

He chuckled and worked me mercilessly, licking and nipping my clit. This time he let me drop over the edge of the cliff. I came so hard I had to bite my lip to keep from screaming.

He finally lifted his shining face from me and grabbed a fistful of hair. He drew my face to his and kissed me. His mouth tasted of the tang of my arousal.

"See how delicious you are?" He kissed me again, tracing around my lips with his tongue.

I reached forward to undo his pants and slide them down his hips. His erection happily sprang free, thick, red and hard. His tip shone with precum.

I raised my legs and pressed my heels into his back, pushing him insistently until his cock slid inside me.

"Pushy omega," he teased.

"Shut up and fuck me, alpha," I growled. "Please," I added sweetly.

"Only because you said please." He grabbed my hips with his large hands and pulled me forward until I was only perched on the edge of the throne. He grunted and thrust into me, slowly at first.

"What is it about you that the more I get, the more I want?" He asked, his voice already breathless with exertion and concentration.

"I'm amazing," I said jokingly. I gripped the hand rests of the throne and used them to roll my hips in time with his.

"Yes, you are," he agreed. "And I'm going to come inside your beautiful, amazing body. If anyone sees us walking back down the corridor, they won't know you have my cum dripping down your thighs."

Gods, yes, please.

I was tempted to make a comment about anyone here in the palace expecting me to have his cum on my face, but instead I concentrated on squeezing my muscles around his cock and driving him to oblivion.

His fingers tightened on my hips. He thrust once, twice more before he came.

He groaned, the sound so deep and compelling it forced another orgasm out of me. This one was quick and shallow, but no less pleasurable than the other.

We held each other and panted for a while before we somehow managed to remember where we were.

We quickly pulled our clothes back together and slipped out of the throne room before anyone knew we were there.

30

KHALA

"I trust you slept well." Harel gave Cavan a meaningful look.

It seemed the guards did their job and told him where we were in the middle of the night. If his expression was any indication, he'd checked and found the replacement key in place.

I'd wanted to leave right after we left the throne room, but Cavan reasoned that nothing said suspicious as fuck like sneaking away in the middle of the night.

"We might need him yet," he'd said.

"If you say so." I thought I was going to get another lecture about, 'When you're as old as I am, you don't burn bridges.'

Instead he smiled and said, "I do say so."

"Do you have to take smug lessons to become High Lord?" I asked. "Or is it something you're born with?"

"It's a skill we hone over time," he said. "We can't be seen to lack confidence or no one will follow us."

"Confidence or arrogance?" I teased.

"Is there a difference?" He grabbed my wrist, pulled me to him and smacked my ass. "That's what you get for questioning your alpha."

"One of them." I twisted around until I was facing him.

He sighed. "Yes, one of them. If it wasn't for that bond, I'd talk you out of any desire to be with Ryze. I'm sure he's as happy to share you with me as I am sharing with him."

"According to Tavian, it's an alpha's job to make sure his omega is happy, regardless of what he has to do to achieve that. Even if that means sharing with someone you don't like. Maybe if you get to know each other..."

"Tavian is right," Cavan conceded. "Liking each other might be a stretch, but we may come to respect each other. In the end, we both want the same thing. A happy, content, satisfied omega. Especially satisfied." He kissed me lightly. "Come on. Let's have breakfast and say our goodbyes."

"Gladly." The sooner we were gone from here, the better.

"I slept very well," Cavan said, his words bringing

me back to the present. "It must have been all the fine wine and company."

"Autumn Court wine is undeniably the best in Jorius or any of the human lands," Harel said.

He said nothing about the company.

"It's very drinkable," Cavan agreed. "I'm glad we were able to come to an understanding as well."

I forced myself not to glance at him. I kept my eyes down on my cereal and sweet tea and tried to contain my curiosity.

Understanding about what? What concessions had he given to Harel to buy me time to look for the key?

"It will be mutually beneficial," Harel said.

Either he didn't want to talk about it in front of me, or he enjoyed being cagey as hells. Maybe both. I'd ask Cavan about it when we left.

"It definitely will," Cavan agreed. "I can return to the Summer Court knowing our alliance is stronger than ever."

"And I can look forward to expanding my lands. For too long, we've been confined to this one corner, while the humans let their lands fall into ruin. It's past time for the Fae to return and rule as we should have been doing."

I almost choked on my mouthful. I coughed a couple of times while Cavan patted my back.

"Does the part-human whore object?" Harel seemed amused.

"Of course not," Cavan said smoothly. "She's Fae now, and knows better than to question her High Lord. Her food just went down the wrong hole for a moment."

Harel grunted and I could almost hear him thinking that I didn't have any wrong holes. All of mine were there for the taking. If not by him, then at least by whomever Cavan gave me to.

"Good," Harel said. "I'd hate to miss seeing the look on her face when the humans kneel to us."

Lucky for everyone, I had one hand in my lap. He couldn't see me curl it into a fist that I wanted to pound into his face. I struggled to keep my body from stiffening. Everything in me wanted to respond, but I couldn't.

I felt a surge of concern from Tavian through the bond. That was what kept me from losing my composure entirely. I sent back thoughts that I was fine.

I managed to take a calming breath and continue eating.

"You may get to see that yet." I felt Cavan's eyes on me, but I ignored them. He was definitely having way, way too much fun with this. I wouldn't rule out using that fist again.

"She's broken, but there are others like her who

aren't," Cavan added. "Not to mention the humans themselves. I'm sure you'll enjoy toying with them."

"In the same way a child likes to play with a puppy," Harel said. "Humans are, after all, nothing more than animals."

"Of course." Cavan set his teacup down on the table. "Now, if you'll excuse me, I need to return to my court."

Evidently, it didn't matter that I wasn't finished. Of course it didn't. It was only a courtesy that I got any food in the first place.

Whatever, as long as we got out of here, I didn't care. I'd have a proper meal later, somewhere a long way from here.

When Cavan stood, I hurried to follow. I managed to avoid looking at Harel. There was no way he'd miss seeing the disgust on my face.

I bit my lip while we walked down the corridor towards the courtyard that led out into the city.

"Don't say anything, we're still being watched," Cavan said, his hand around my upper arm. "Something is wrong."

It certainly was, but I managed to contain myself for a while longer.

I thought we'd portal out from the courtyard, but we kept walking out into the city.

"He put wards in place to stop me from opening a

portal," Cavan said in my ear. Anyone overhearing, would have assumed he was growling at me.

"You, or anyone?" I asked.

Hopefully I managed to look like I was scared of him. Truthfully I was scared, because his tone put me on edge. We'd come this far. Being stopped now would be frustrating as hells. Not to mention potentially deadly.

"I don't know, the wards feel strange. I can't put my finger on it. It's not like anything I've felt before."

"Should we get inside somewhere?" I asked.

He glanced at me, then nodded. He all but pulled me over to a tall inn, and through the front door. He pushed me over towards a table, then turned to look out the window, firmly putting himself between me and anything out there.

"Do you see anything?" I stood behind him and ignored the stares of the patrons eating breakfast.

He shook his head slightly. "Nothing, but it still feels wrong. I don't think it's autumn magic doing that. Don't use any of your own. In case they're looking for it."

I didn't need to ask who 'they' were. If this was something new to him, then chances were it was related to one of the lost courts.

"They don't want us leaving with the key," I whispered.

"That would be my guess," he said. "Either Illaria told them, or someone else did. The map in Havenmoor wouldn't tell you anything unless you already knew."

"Who else knows?" I asked. "You, Ryze, Harel, Illaria. Tavian, Vayne and Zared."

"Ryze's designated heir, Johah," Cavan said softly. "I don't have one. And then only Thiron and—"

"His heir, Wornar," I said as Wornar stepped through the crowds out on the street, and moved towards the inn.

"And him," Cavan agreed.

"Fuck," I said softly.

"Potentially," Cavan agreed.

"If he betrayed us, can I rip his head off?" I asked.

"Certainly, but wait for my go-ahead. This might not be what we think it is."

"Excuse me if I don't take that bet," I said dryly.

Wornar stepped through the door to the inn and nodded at us.

"I apologise for sidetracking you both, but I believe you have something I need."

"Oh really?" Cavan asked. "What might that be?" He crossed his arms and kept himself between me and the Spring Court Fae.

"You can try to pretend you don't know, but we both know you do," Wornar said.

"Humour me," Cavan said. He looked completely unmoved.

"The key to Nallis." Wornar's tone was as friendly as ever, although his eyes spoke of his impatience.

"What about it?" I asked.

"I know you have it," he said.

"So what if we do?" Cavan asked. "What would you need it for? Are you planning to open the place yourself?"

"It doesn't matter what I need it for," he said. "Only that I need it and you have it." He held out his hand. "No one needs to get hurt here today."

"I don't know about that," I said. "You're here demanding a key we may or may not have, and you're not telling us why. If you're so sure we have it, then you'd know the reason for that. If you do, then you wouldn't want to stop us."

Wornar stepped around Cavan, who moved to keep himself between us. He grunted softly.

"That might be exactly why I'm here. To keep anyone from opening that place."

"Why?" I asked. "It seems to me the sooner we deal with those courts, the better."

"Or we can keep them contained where they are," Wornar said. "Thiron agrees it's better to leave them alone. He wants me to get the keys so we can hide them. We'll find a way to stop them from waking."

"Unless you haven't been paying attention, it's already started," Cavan said. "Our best allies against the shadows might be the Court of Dreams."

Wornar shook his head. "Thiron doesn't want to take the risk. Give me the key."

"No," Cavan said.

"Then you leave me no choice," Wornar said. He looked around at me and said, "Take his knife and slide it between his ribs."

I shook my head and tried to back away, but the alpha-order settled on me. I didn't even have time to fight it before I was slipping Cavan's knife out from the sheath at his hip and driving it into him.

Warm blood spurted over my hand, coating my fingers. I let out a sob.

Gods, no, no, no.

My eyes were wide, staring. This couldn't be happening. None of it. I felt like I was watching myself through the eyes of someone else.

But I wasn't. I had done this. Me, because being an omega meant I had to obey.

Somehow...somehow this was all my fault.

Cavan's eyes widened in surprise and pain. His knees started to buckle.

Wornar grabbed him and held him up long enough to slip his hands into his pockets. He searched for a few moments until he turned up the key.

"Let the hilt of the knife go and come with me," he ordered.

Hot tears ran down my face. Every part of me was screaming not to do what he wanted me to do. My movements stiff and tight, I moved towards Wornar.

"Asshole," I ground out.

"Quiet," he ordered. His words were like a choker around my throat.

I tried to growl and found I couldn't even do that.

I was a Silent Maiden again.

Cavan dropped to his knees, his hand around the blade of the knife. His fingers were covered in blood. Eyes wide with pain and fury.

I could only mouth his name before the order forced me to follow Wornar out the door.

THANK YOU FOR READING! The story continues in Sword of Balm and Shadow. If you'd like a bonus scene of Khala visiting Tyla, you can get that here.

ABOUT THE AUTHOR

Maggie Alabaster writes reverse harem and, paranormal, sci-fi and fantasy romance.

She lives in NSW, Australia with one spouse, two daughters, one dog, and countless birds.

Sign up for Maggie's newsletter! Sign Up!

Join Maggie's reader group! Join here!

Follow Maggie on Bookbub! Click here to follow me!

Check out Maggie's website- www.maggiealabaster.com

ALSO BY MAGGIE ALABASTER

Brutal Academy

Book 1 Heartless

Book 2 Cruel

Book 3 Vengeful

Court of Blood and Binding

Book 1 Song of Scent and Magic

Book 2 Crown of Mist and Heat

Book 3 Sword of Balm and Shadow

Book 4 Whisper of Frost and Flame

Dark Masque

Book 1 Bait

Book 2 Prey

Book 3 Trap

Saving Abbie

Book 1 Pitch

Book 2 Pound

Book 3 Session

Book 4 Muse

Book 5 Rhythm

Book 6 Encore

Novella Venomous

Saving Abbie books 1-4

Saving Abbie books 4-6 + Venomous

Ruthless Claws

Book 1 Ivory

Book 2 Crimson

Book 3 Elodie

Harmony's Magic

Book 1 Summoned by Fire

Book 2 Summoned by Fate

Book 3 Summoned by Desire

Shifter's Vault

Book 1 Discarded

Book 2 Deceived

Book 3 Disgraced

My Alien Mates

Book 1 Star Warriors

www.ingramcontent.com/pod-product-compliance
Lightning Source LLC
Chambersburg PA
CBHW020329120726
47904CB00002B/346